CROSSFIRE

JAMES P. SUMNER

BOTH
barrels
PUBLISHING

CROSSFIRE

THIRD EDITION PUBLISHED IN 2022 BY BOTH BARRELS PUBLISHING LTD.

EDITING AND COVER DESIGN BY: BOTHBARRELSAUTHORSERVICES.COM

ISBNs:
978-1-914191-29-9 (HARDBACK)
978-1-914191-30-5 (PAPERBACK)

VISIT THE AUTHOR'S WEBSITE: JAMESPSUMNER.COM

JOIN THE MAILING LIST

Why not sign up for James P. Sumner's spam-free newsletter, and stay up-to-date with the latest news, promotions, and new releases?

In exchange for your support, you will receive a **FREE** copy of the prequel novella, *A Hero of War*, which tells the story of a young Adrian, newly recruited to the U.S. Army at the beginning of the Gulf War.

Previously available on Amazon, this title is now exclusive to the author's website. But you have the opportunity to read it for free!

Interested? Details can be found at the end of this book.

Welcome to the Thrillerverse...

PREVIOUSLY...

On April 22, 2017, GlobaTech Industries sent a small unit of elite soldiers from its own private military force to Prague. Their mission was to apprehend a man carrying information that proved a conspiracy at the highest levels of U.S. government.

The mission was organized and executed under the supervision of Josh Winters, a former soldier and special operative, and Ryan Schultz, the acting CEO of GlobaTech Industries at the time.

The team was successful but were involved in an unexpected and unavoidable skirmish with a unit of mercenaries recently disavowed by the CIA. There was collateral damage, both physical and political. With GlobaTech's position as the acting peacekeeping force for the United Nations, coupled with the growing tension inside the government, there was demand from the public for someone to blame. Ryan Schultz and Josh Winters were left with little choice but to terminate the employment of their elite unit, painting them as enemies in the eyes of the world and using them as scapegoats for what happened in Prague.

Shortly after this, the assassin known as Adrian Hell shot and killed U.S. President Charles Cunningham inside the Oval Office. In the aftermath, Ryan Schultz was sworn in as his successor at the request of the Secretary of State.

A few weeks later, Josh Winters was shot and killed by an unknown assailant on a street corner in Rome.

That was two years ago.

PROLOGUE

The chorus of crickets echoed in the silence, hidden in the tall, dry grass beside the dirt road. The temperature was in the low eighties, despite the late hour, and the breeze that drifted in from the Mexican coast did little to counter the evening heat.

Two shadows crouched in the undergrowth, motionless and calm, watching the single-story brick house opposite. Its walls were cracked from years of neglect. The tiles on the roof were loose in places, and the frail wooden shutters stood open at the windows, allowing light to flood out and bathe the dusty street in its orange glow.

The car had arrived ten minutes ago, parking haphazardly on the makeshift driveway to the right of the entrance. Two men had climbed out, moving quickly to the trunk and lifting the small child out of it. It was a girl no older than eight. Duct tape covered her mouth and bound her wrists and ankles. Her face was dirty and stained with tears. Her clothes were torn in places. The faint wind blew the loose material, which quietly flapped against her body.

The taller of the two men had heaved the girl over his

shoulder, carrying her into the house with ease. The other man had looked up and down the street before following his partner inside and slamming the door shut. There had been no sound or movement since.

One of the shadows stood, flexing its enormous frame and adjusting its grip on the silenced assault rifle it held. It set off walking, cautiously placing one large boot in front of the other. The sound of them brushing through the grass was interrupted by a crunch underfoot, which silenced the noise of the insects. The shadow froze momentarily, waiting for any sign its presence was known... but there was nothing.

It continued, more carefully than before, and soon drew level with the house. The shadow dropped to one knee again, sinking back into the darkness against the low wall that separated the road from the cliffside, which dropped down to the bay. The assault rifle was aimed forward, the barrel always following the eyes, ready for anything.

"In position," said Jericho Stone into his comms unit.

"Copy that, Jerry," replied Ray Collins. "Making my move."

The second shadow emerged from cover and crossed the road, quick and low. Light from the window partially illuminated Collins's face as he crouched against the far side of the car, hidden once more from his targets.

Collins rested his weapon against his leg and fumbled with the cover on the gas tank. He pried it open and unscrewed the cap, then retrieved a dirty rag from his back pocket. He pushed the rag inside, soaking it in gasoline, then wiped it along the side of the car, allowing the excess liquid to drip onto the ground. Standing quietly, he walked toward the front door of the house, leaving a thin trail of fuel behind him. He dropped the rag at the side of the single step, dried his hand on his leg, and then moved across the front, taking cover on the opposite side of the building, directly opposite Jericho. Collins looked over at the darkness, knowing his partner was hidden within.

"All set, Jerry," he whispered.

Jericho inched forward, revealing himself in the dull glow of the night. "Let's get her back."

Collins made his way along the side of the house and paused beside the back door. Jericho crossed the narrow street and pressed his back against the wall beneath the open window. Using his thick, powerful legs, he cautiously stood so that his head was level with the rotted ledge. He took a deep breath and held it before flashing a split-second glance through the gap in the shutters. He dropped back into cover almost instantly, his trained eye seeing everything he needed to.

"Ray, I have eyes on four hostiles at the front of the house," he said quietly. "No sign of the girl—she must be in another room somewhere."

Collins moved into position, mirroring Jericho near the back door. He flicked a glance through the window, into the kitchen.

"Yeah, I've got her," he replied in his low, gravelly Irish tone. "Two hostiles, one either side of her, sitting at a table."

"Okay. Moving into position by the door. We breach on three. Quick and clean. Ready?"

"When you are, Jerry. One..."

"Two..."

"T'ree!"

Collins stood and kicked the door hard, just to the side of the handle. It flew open, and he stormed into the kitchen, firing two controlled, accurate bursts in quick succession. Each one caught a man in the chest. The girl's eyes went

3

wide with alarm; her involuntary scream was nothing more than a muffle against the duct tape.

From the other side of the house, Collins heard four bursts of suppressed gunfire—three in quick succession and one a few seconds later, which interrupted a man's yell.

Knowing Jericho had everything covered, he let his gun hang loose and hurried toward the girl, putting a finger to his lips and gesturing for her to stay calm.

"Hey, it's okay," he said to her. "We're gonna get ya outta here, I promise."

Her body relaxed back in her chair as she took deep breaths through her nose. Collins looked into her large, innocent eyes, trying to imagine what it must be like for a child that age to experience such horror.

"I'm gonna take this tape off your mouth, all right? It's gonna sting a little bit, but I need ya to be brave and stay quiet, okay?"

She nodded silently, not taking her wide eyes off him.

He moved his hand gently to her face, wiping a tear away with his thumb as he pinched one corner of the tape.

A sudden burst of gunfire from behind made him flinch, and he instinctively ducked, pulling the tape straight off as he did. The girl couldn't hold in the yelp of pain and surprise. As he dropped to one knee, he spun around, grabbing his rifle and taking aim.

Jericho stood in the doorway, his gun raised, smoke whirling from the barrel. Next to the doorway opposite, a man with a knife in his hand slowly slid down the wall, leaving a long, crimson stain behind him.

"Heh... thanks, Jerry. I owe ya one."

"I'll add it to the list," he replied, shrugging. "Are we good here?"

Collins looked at the girl, who nodded at him silently

before throwing her small arms around his neck. He stood, scooping her up and holding her in his left arm. She wrapped her short, bruised legs around him and buried her face in his shoulder.

He turned, holding his gun ready in his right hand. "Aye, we're good. Let's get the hell outta Dodge before anyone else arrives."

Jericho walked with purpose back through the house, toward the front door. Collins followed behind him, moving slow, checking their six.

They stepped out onto the road, scanning both ways before crossing and crouching low in the undergrowth against the wall opposite.

Jericho placed a finger to his ear, activating his comms unit. "Jules, what's your position?"

There was a crackle of static, and Julie Fisher's voice came on the line. She sounded flustered, and her voice was loud because of background noise. "I'm coming to you now... maybe three minutes out. Gimme some good news, boys."

"We've got the girl," announced Jericho.

"Casualties?"

"Seven. All armed hostiles."

"Ah, crap!" interrupted Collins. "Jerry, we've got company."

The dirt road was on a slight rise, which dropped away and curved left approximately a mile and half to the west. Two sets of headlights sped toward them in the distance, approaching the bend.

"I see them," said Jericho. "Julie, we have two vehicles, maybe ninety seconds out."

"You need to hold them off," replied Julie. "I ran into

some trouble myself back here, and it delayed me. Whoever's coming will reach you before I do."

"Copy that," said Jericho. He looked up at Collins. "Ray, you got a light?"

Kneeling in front of the young girl, Collins rested his rifle against the wall next to her and reached into his pocket. He pulled out a rusted silver Zippo, which he tossed over to his partner.

"Heh... ya picked a helluva time to start smokin', Jerry."

"Nah, I've got enough bad habits for the both of us already," he replied, smiling as he stood and headed back across the road, toward the house.

Collins retrieved his gun and looked at the girl. "He's right—smoking's real bad for ya, kid, but it's better than getting shot at. Trust me."

The girl giggled. "You're funny!"

"Aye, kid—funny-*lookin'*! Stay quiet for a sec, 'kay?" Collins looked to his right at the approaching cars. "Jerry, how we doin' there, matey?"

Jericho moved around the hood of the car, letting his rifle hang loose as he placed both hands flat on it. Scuffing his boots on the ground to secure his footing, he leaned forward at a forty-five-degree angle. The muscles on his hulking frame bulged as he pushed the car down the driveway and into the middle of the road.

Once it was in place, he looked over at Collins. "I'm good. Now let's move."

Collins picked up the girl again and sprinted to his left, away from the house and the oncoming cars. As soon as they were clear, Jericho tossed the lighter onto the rag at the side of the step and ran after them. Moving fast, they linked up and continued to run until they reached the clearing in the undergrowth where they had started almost ten minutes earlier. They turned and watched as the flame chased along the dripped line of gasoline like a starving beast. It followed the car as it rolled slowly across the dirt track.

Seconds later, it reached the gas tank, and a thunderous explosion rang out, propelling the car straight up into the air. The smell of burning fuel was strong, and the initial blast lit up the night sky. The flaming remains of the car landed with a loud, metallic thump, blocking the road ahead. Despite the distance, they had to squint as the heat touched their faces.

"Beautiful!" said Collins, laughing. He looked at the girl in his arms. She had her eyes screwed tightly shut and her hands over her ears. He bounced her up and down gently to get her attention. She opened one eye and smiled. "What's your name, kiddo?"

"Jessica," she whispered.

He held up his hand, and she high-fived him.

"Well, Jessie—I'm just gonna call ya Jessie, okay?—I gotta say... you're pretty badass, d'ya know that?"

She giggled and wrapped her arms around his neck, burying her face in his shoulder as they slowed to a walk.

Jericho noticed the way Collins was with her—how natural he appeared at reassuring her and keeping her safe. The two of them had known each other a number of years, yet he had never seen that side of his friend. It wasn't unusual for Collins to have a different female companion seemingly every weekend, though what he lacked in decency, he more than made up for in charm. Yet, seeing him with a child, Jericho noticed a natural father figure in him, which came as a pleasant surprise.

"Come on," he urged them. "That barricade won't hold them for long. Julie, where are you?"

"Not far," she replied. "I'm assuming that fire I see is your handiwork?"

Jericho exchanged a glance with Collins and smiled. "Yeah, we didn't want you to miss us in the dark."

Moments later, headlights illuminated the road in front of them. They were dim at first but gradually brightened until a black Range Rover slid into view, stopping beside them. Jericho reached for the passenger door and climbed in. Collins followed suit, holding the rear door open for the girl, who climbed inside eagerly.

"Scooch over, Princess," he said, diving in beside her.

The doors slammed shut, and Julie hit the gas. The rear end fish-tailed in the gravel as she accelerated back the way she came, checking her rear view for anyone in pursuit. She ran a hand habitually over her auburn hair, which was tied back in a loose ponytail. Her gray tank-top was patchy with sweat, and her bare arms were tense as she drove.

Happy they were clear, she glanced sideways at Jericho and sighed. "Do either of you know the meaning of the word *discreet*?"

Behind her, Jessie tapped Collins on the shoulder and leaned in close, whispering in his ear. "She sounds really mad..."

Collins chuckled. "Yeah, kid, she always gets mad when we blow stuff up. But we got ya back safe and sound, so I reckon she'll forgive us. Just this once."

Julie looked quickly over her shoulder and saw the girl had curled up in a ball and tucked herself into Collins' side. She turned her attention to him and smiled before looking back at the road.

"It's only a half-mile to the docks," she announced. "Our boat's waiting for us."

Jericho rested a hand on the dash, steadying himself against the suspension as they raced across the uneven road.

"Did you say you hit some trouble on your way in?" he asked her.

She nodded without taking her eyes off the road. "A Jeep came up on me out of nowhere. Two guys in the back were taking pot-shots at me all the way up from the coast. It's as if they knew where to find me."

Collins leaned forward slightly, resting an arm on the back of her seat. "D'ya think we slipped up somewhere? Maybe our client sold us out?"

Jericho shook his head. "Not likely. He wouldn't endanger the life of his daughter by telling her kidnappers we were coming. The way I figure it, this is Mexico. Someone snatches a kid and brings them here... doesn't matter who's behind it. There's always somebody higher up the food chain you gotta clear it with. Best guess, one of the cartels had look-outs and made us the second we came into port."

Julie slammed her palm on the wheel. "We should've been more careful..."

Jericho nudged her arm gently with his hand. "Don't be so hard on yourself, Jules. Bottom line, we came here, rescued the girl, and we're getting out again. We did our job and handled the drama."

"Amen," said Collins, smiling.

Julie sighed. "Yeah, you're right. I just don't like—"

Another car appeared from their left at speed and smashed nose-first into the rear side of their vehicle. The collision was deafening. Julie wrestled with the wheel as they spun counter-clockwise across the road, the tires locked and scraping loudly on the gravel.

"Shit!" she yelled.

They came to an abrupt halt as the passenger side of the Range Rover hit the wide, thick trunk of a tree. Jericho flew against his door and Julie into him. On the rear seat, Collins instinctively dove sideways to cover the girl with his body, trying to minimize the effects of the impact on her small frame. Hunched over, his shoulders and upper back slammed against the door. He grunted and fell forward, putting his hands out so as not to crush the girl with his weight.

The sounds of twisting metal and chaos faded. The engine died. Silence fell. Julie pushed off Jericho and sat back in her seat, blinking hard and often to re-focus. Jericho adjusted himself and did the same.

Collins pushed himself up off the seat and looked at the girl. Her eyes were screwed tightly shut, and her hands were over her ears. She was curled into a ball, lying on her side. He carefully placed a hand on her arm.

"Hey, Jessie, you're safe now. It's over." His touch startled her, and she screamed as she snapped her eyes open. He backed away, holding his hands up. "Hey, hey, it's all right. Shush now. I'm here for ya."

She fell silent, taking deep breaths. Collins moved over and sat back in his seat, grimacing as the impact stung his shoulders. "Everyone okay?"

"Yeah, I think we're good," replied Jericho before nodding toward the girl. "How is she?"

Collins glanced sideways. Jessie was sitting straight, staring blankly ahead.

"She's fine," he said. "I think she might be going into shock, but it's nothing we can't deal with. Physically, she's as good as we could hope for. Jules, what the hell happened?"

Julie stared at the wheel, still feeling a little dazed. "I

don't know. That other car, it... it came from nowhere. I didn't see it."

Jericho placed a hand gently on her leg, patting it to offer some comfort. "Don't worry about it. Everyone here is okay, which is what matters. I'm gonna go check on the other car, see if anyone was injured."

He pushed open his door, which required some force as it was misshapen from the crash. He climbed out and quickly looked around. The car that had hit them had stopped just a few yards farther along the road, side-on so that it covered both lanes. As Jericho began walking toward it, all four doors of the other car swung open in unison. Men emerged holding automatic weapons.

The scene momentarily froze. The men slowly took their aim as Jericho processed what was happening, trying to comprehend that the crash clearly wasn't an accident. A noise behind him snapped him back to reality. He turned to see Julie opening her door and climbing out of their vehicle. He waved her back.

"Get down!" he managed to shout as the bullets began to fly.

The staccato roar of gunfire filled the air. Jericho instinctively dropped to the ground in a spin and scrambled back behind the Range Rover, desperate to find cover.

Julie dove back inside and pressed herself against the front seats, placing her hands over her head. In the back, Collins once again threw his body over Jessie, sliding them both as low as he could into the footwells. The hail of bullets seemed never-ending, and the noise was interrupted only by the repetitive dull *thunk* as another round made a hole in the bodywork of their vehicle.

Jericho scurried on his front toward the wreck of their Range Rover. "Julie! Weapon!"

A moment later, his FN SCAR-L rifle slid across the gravel toward him from under the open door. He wrapped his hand around the polymer stock as he struggled to his feet and sought cover behind the car. Bullets kicked up countless plumes of dust around his feet as he ran. He slid around the crumpled hood like a baseball player and crouched low, slamming his shoulder against the fender. He checked the mag, flicked off the safety, and held his weapon ready, waiting for his moment.

Collins stared at his own rifle as he shielded Jessie. It was resting on the floor in the foot-well, behind the passenger seat. He reached for it and pushed it through the gap between the two front seats.

"Here, Jules," he shouted as he rested it beside her. "Use this and give 'em hell—I hate getting shot at!"

She twisted on the seats, keeping as low as she could, and grabbed the rifle. She instinctively went through the same routine Jericho had: checking the mag, flicking the safety off, and adjusting her grip, ready for action.

She turned onto her back and shuffled down, so her legs rested over the edge of the driver's seat.

"Jericho, where are you?" she called out.

"Getting ready to shoot these assholes," he replied. "You?"

"Ditto. On three?"

"Count it."

Julie took a deep breath. "One..."

"Two..." said Jericho.

"Three!"

Using her lower legs for leverage, she sat up and leaned out, moving her rifle around the frame of the car and taking aim. She opened fire at the exact second Jericho did. They both took their shots expertly and efficiently, timing their controlled bursts and hitting three of the four men between them in the first few seconds.

The remaining assailant, who was farthest away from them and shielded by his own vehicle, dropped out of sight. An unnerving silence descended on the area, broken only by the sound of three lifeless bodies slumping heavily to the ground.

"On me." Jericho moved out of cover and across the road, his body partly crouched, his weapon aiming forward, finger hovering over the trigger.

Julie circled away from the crash site, moving across the road to provide cover from the opposite angle.

As they approached, the remaining man popped up, screaming. Before he had a chance to fire, Julie and Jericho each unloaded another short, controlled burst, both hitting him in the chest. He flailed backward, sending his weapon flying away from him.

"Clear," said Julie.

"Clear," confirmed Jericho.

A moment later, Collins appeared beside them, holding the girl with one hand as she wrapped her arms around his neck and buried her face into his shoulder. They both turned and nodded to him.

He glanced around the area before looking at each of them in turn. "Can we *please* get the hell outta here now?"

"I'd love to," replied Julie, "but our ride's totaled."

Jericho pointed along the road ahead of them, which stretched away to their right and out of sight around a bend. "It can't be more than a mile or so to the coast. Maybe not even that. Our boat's there, waiting for us. I say we stick to the edges and make our way on foot. We've already taken out... what? Ten guys? We stopped two more vehicles full of assholes back at the house, but they might be working their way around to us. We can't afford to waste time staying in one place while we wait for an emergency evac."

Julie nodded. "Agreed. Bottom line, we have the daughter back, but I'll bet my last dime there are more people en route."

Collins looked at Jessie, who had her eyes closed. He smiled, amazed at the difference between an adult's mind and a child's mind. Despite having been kidnapped and stuck in the middle of a gunfight, the eight-year-old girl had managed to fall asleep, no doubt drained from the stress. A small puddle of saliva stained the shoulder of his shirt.

He smiled to himself and whispered, "That is badass..."

Julie nodded to him. "You ready?"

"Aye, let's go. I'll leave the shooting to the two of ya, if it's all the same."

Jericho smiled, turned on his heels, and set off walking, holding his rifle up and resting it on his shoulder. As Collins followed, Julie moved alongside him.

"It suits you, y'know?" she said, smiling. "Being a father figure."

Collins rolled his eyes. "Hey, less of that kinda talk, lady. I've a reputation to maintain."

She nudged his arm playfully. "Your secret's safe with me, jackass."

She pushed the pace to catch up with Jericho, and the three of them walked on, the crunch of their boots on the dirt road the only sound.

CROSSFIRE
GLOBATECH: BOOK 2

1

September 25, 2019

Moses Buchanan stood with his arms folded across his barrel chest. Resting against the edge of his desk, he stared patiently at the large video conferencing screen mounted on the wall in front of him. He looked younger than his years, a testament to his disciplined approach to exercise—a mindset instilled in him long ago, during his time serving in the Special Forces. His skin was black as coal, and his voice boomed with a natural, smooth growl.

"Mr. Hyatt, if you would let me explain," he said.

The man on the TV screen shook his head furiously. "I paid you a small fortune to protect my daughter. Not only did you allow her to be taken, but you put her in the middle of a *gunfight*! What the hell kind of operation are you running over there?"

"Mr. Hyatt, please..." Buchanan pushed himself away from his desk and paced slowly toward the screen, clasping his hands behind his back. "Your daughter is safe, which is our primary—"

"She *was* safe! Then you let her get kidnapped!"

Buchanan ground his teeth until his jaw hurt, suppressing his growing frustration. When he replied, he spoke firmly.

"And then we got her back. And for the record, we didn't *let* anything happen to her. Bad people—which you neglected to mention might be a factor, I hasten to add—ambushed our security team and took her, killing four of my men in the process. I had to send a specialist unit into Mexico to get your daughter back alive—which they did, at great physical risk to themselves."

The man on the screen fell silent. Ulysses Hyatt sat behind a desk in his own office, some three thousand miles away in Montreal. He wore a shirt with an open collar, his tie loosened around his neck. He looked disheveled and sleep-deprived. Bloodshot eyes stared unblinking into the camera at Buchanan. He didn't respond but simply nodded once, conceding the man's point.

Buchanan continued. "Mr. Hyatt, I understand this is a difficult time for you, but you hired us to protect your family, and we *are* doing so, to the very best of our ability."

When Hyatt finally spoke, his tone was much quieter and more subdued than before.

"How is my baby girl?"

Buchanan relaxed and smiled. "Little Jessica's fine. Our medical team checked her over when she arrived back here about an hour ago. We have contacts who work in the U.S. government's Witness Protection Program, and we're moving her to a safe house later today. She will be under twenty-four-hour watch for as long as you need, at no extra cost to you."

Hyatt stood and moved around his desk, sitting on the edge, leaning close to the camera. He let out a tired breath. "Thank you. I... I appreciate you giving my case your personal attention, and... and I'm sorry for my outburst earlier."

Buchanan figured the apology wasn't easy, so he swallowed his own pride and waved his hand dismissively. "Water under the bridge, Mr. Hyatt. You're under a lot of pressure, and I can't begin to imagine what you're going through. I'm just glad we can take one of those concerns away from you. Now, if you need anything else, you call me, okay?"

Hyatt nodded. "Actually, there is something. I have a meeting in a few days, which I'm hoping will signal the end of this current business deal and the trouble that's gone along with it. I'm happy my daughter is safe, but after the attempt to kidnap her, I fear my own life will now be on the line until this is concluded."

"You need personal protection," said Buchanan. It was an observation, not a question.

"I'll pay extra, of course."

"I will send two of my very best. They can be with you as early as this evening."

Hyatt's body relaxed. His shoulders slumped forward as he exhaled heavily with relief. "Thank you, Mr. Buchanan. I really do appreciate everything that you're doing."

"All part of the service. My people will be in touch." He reached for the remote beside him and clicked off the screen, terminating the call. He sighed. "Asshole."

He sat in his chair and spun it around to gaze out the window. The late morning sun beamed down, bright and pale, shining through the glass and challenging his air conditioning. He leaned back and let out another sigh, massaging the bridge of his nose between his index finger and thumb. He felt exhausted, and these brief moments of reprieve, where he could simply stare out of the window in silence, mindlessly watching the world pass by, were all that kept him going over the last couple of months.

Buchanan had been elected as the new CEO of Globa-Tech Industries shortly after the murder of Josh Winters. It wasn't a position he had ever considered for himself and certainly wasn't one he wanted, given the circumstances of his promotion.

He had served in the Green Berets, as part of the 1st Special Forces Group until the late nineties. He was forced to retire from active duty after taking a bullet to the hip during a routine patrol in Iraq. Despite making a full recovery following surgery, his long-term mobility was affected, and he never received medical clearance to return to the field. Feeling he still had a few good years left in him, he used his payout to set up his own private security firm. His goal was simply to provide an affordable service to people who needed help.

He knew many private companies preferred to specialize in one particular area, with personal security and bail enforcement being the two main fields. He wanted his company to do it all, and he knew with his training and his selective recruitment process, he could deliver any type of security service he was asked for.

With the economy in decline, he struggled financially, eventually relenting and selling his company to GlobaTech in the summer of 2002. He was assigned a senior position overseeing logistics for their own security force, which back then was only a quarter of the size it is today.

He was dedicated, passionate about his job, and successful in every way possible. Shortly after 4/17, when

Josh Winters took control of the company following Ryan Schultz's impromptu election to President, Buchanan was called up to serve as one of Josh's top advisors. Between them, they continued to reinforce GlobaTech's presence, establishing them as not only America's but the world's peacekeeping force. They were free from Congressional oversight, financially self-reliant, and thanks to their efforts stopping former president Charles Cunningham's terrorist plot, GlobaTech quickly became the largest and most powerful company on the planet.

He had adapted well to his new role and responsibilities, but that took nothing away from how difficult his life had become. That's why moments like this one, where he could sit, lost in his own thoughts, were so precious to him.

Ulysses Hyatt had made contact a little over a week ago. He had explained he was going through a difficult and troubling time at work, and he had reason to believe the safety of his daughter might be in jeopardy. He paid top dollar to hire a team of private security experts from GlobaTech to protect her for the next few weeks, until his current business was concluded. However, the team Buchanan had assigned to the detail was attacked and killed, and the daughter was taken to Mexico. Ransom demands had been made less than twelve hours later.

Hyatt didn't feel comfortable involving the police, so Buchanan sent a small elite unit to Mexico to retrieve the girl at all costs. They had been successful but not without attracting a little attention along the way. Now he was waiting for them to arrive, so they could deliver their report.

The intercom on his desk buzzed, disturbing him from his brief moment of respite. He spun around and pressed the flashing button. It was his secretary, Kim Mitchell.

"Yeah?"

"They're here, Mr. Buchanan," she replied professionally.

"Thanks, Kim. Send them in, would you?"

A moment later, the door to his office opened. Julie Fisher walked in, with her head held high and a confidence in her step earned through hard experience. Behind her, Ray Collins sauntered in with a smile on his face, followed by Jericho Stone, who stooped slightly as he entered, then closed the door behind him. They lined up in front of Buchanan, standing casually.

The three of them were regarded among the very best GlobaTech employed. When the incident involving President Cunningham was over, Josh Winters was forced to terminate their employment due to political pressures. The climate at the time called for a scapegoat, and these three were it.

Buchanan had worked closely with Fisher and Collins on many occasions over the years, and Jericho had made quite the impact too, when he was recruited straight out of the CIA. His first act as CEO was to reinstate the three of them, reforming the unit that had seen many successes in the past.

He eyed each of them individually before speaking. "Well?"

Jericho took a small step forward, distancing himself slightly from the others. He was a mountain of a man, standing at six-five, with a body that looked chiseled out of granite. His muscles were natural, toned over many years of military service and combat missions, and bulging against the fabric of his clothes. His arms were adorned with tattoos.

He cleared his throat. "Mr. Buchanan, Ray and myself received intel on the location of the girl from one of our contacts in Mexico. We approached the building and counted six hostiles inside, all armed. The girl was in the back room."

"I went around back," added Collins. "Took out the two bastards guardin' her."

"I got the four at the front," continued Jericho. "And a seventh who was hiding in a back room."

Collins nodded. "Yeah, and then we went outside and saw two trucks heading our way. Could've been anywhere up to eight more bad guys heading for us. It's as if they knew we were there, man."

Jericho gestured at Julie with his thumb. "And then Fisher appeared in the Range Rover, said she hit some trouble on the way up from the coast."

Julie nodded. "A Jeep full of assholes appeared out of nowhere, boss, shooting at me, trying to run me off the road. Thankfully, I managed to shake them without too much fuss."

Collins said, "So, we hightailed it out of there, yeah, and then *bam!*" He smacked his fist into his palm. "We got T-boned by *another* car full of gun-toting dick-bags."

"We took *them* out," explained Jericho, "but our ride was a wreck, so we walked the last half-mile back to the coast and hopped on the boat home."

"That's eleven men," said Julie. "And potentially eight more, all for one little girl. Something doesn't add up. Whatever our client is doing, there's more to it than he's letting on. I can't shake the feeling that whoever took her knew we were coming."

Buchanan stroked the coarse stubble along his jawline thoughtfully, staring for a moment at the surface of his desk. He didn't doubt a word they were saying, and the soldier in him was proud of their actions.

Finally, he looked at each of them in turn. "I agree—there's more to this than our client's telling us, but that's not our concern. Our job was to protect that girl at all costs, and despite what we've been up against, we've done an exceptional job. If I were to guess, I would say there's no underlying conspiracy here. What you experienced was simply how things work when you deal with the cartels. They're organized, and they have more manpower and influence than most governments. You did an excellent job of getting out of there. Just... try not to kill so many people next time, okay? I've got a phone call later with the Chief of Federal Police, who's spent most of the early hours of today processing a shit-ton of dead bodies in his country. That's not the kind of publicity this company needs, no matter how justified it might have been. Non-lethal takedowns aren't anything to be ashamed of, clear?"

They all nodded and muttered their understanding. The room fell silent for a moment, and Collins opened his mouth to speak but caught his words. Buchanan spotted it.

"What is it, Ray?" he asked.

Collins smiled sheepishly, embarrassed his hesitation hadn't gone unnoticed. "How's she doing, boss? Jessie..."

"She's doing fine," he replied. "A little dehydrated and very tired, but she's okay. A tough young lady, by all accounts."

Collins nodded. "Aye, she kicked ass, Mr. B."

Buchanan smiled. "The way I hear it, she made a new friend out there."

Collins cast a glance sideways at Julie, who winked back at him.

"I have two people with her now," Buchanan continued. "As soon as she's been given the all clear by our medical personnel, they're going to take her to a safe house we're borrowing from WITSEC until this whole thing blows over."

He got to his feet and walked around his desk, standing in front of his employees. He was average height, marginally taller than Julie and marginally shorter than Collins. Jericho towered over him, as he did with most people.

"So, our client has asked for an additional service," he told them. "He has a business deal nearing completion, which he hopes will put an end to whatever he's involved in that's been endangering his family. He's asked for some personal protection. I've told him it's a two-person job. Who wants it?"

"Where's the gig?" asked Julie.

"Montreal. The plane leaves in a few hours. Hotel will be booked en route, and you'll be there for a couple of days. Maybe three, at the most."

Collins raised his hand. "If, ah... if it's all right with the two of ya," he nodded to Julie and Jericho, "I wouldn't mind sitting this one out. I've got some vacation time due, and I could use a few days of not being shot at." He turned to Buchanan. "If that's okay, boss?"

Buchanan shrugged. "If you say you need a few days, you won't hear any arguments from me."

Collins subtly punched the air. "Yes! You're the best, boss man."

Buchanan turned to the others. "Is that okay with the pair of you?"

Jericho and Julie exchanged a glance and nodded to each other.

"Fine by us," said Julie. "I've always wanted to go to Canada anyway."

Jericho looked at her, frowning. "Really?"

She shrugged. "Yeah, why not?"

"I mean, you've never been?"

She shook her head. "South Dakota, born and raised. If I ever left the States, it was to go much farther afield than Canada—and usually to shoot people."

He smiled. "Fair enough."

Buchanan clapped his hands together. "Excellent. Operating money will be wired to your accounts. See Kim on your way out for flight details."

The two of them thanked him, bumped fists with Collins, and left the office.

Buchanan moved back around his desk and sat back down again. He looked up at Collins. "So, what do you intend to do with your free time, Ray?"

Collins thought about it for a moment. "Not figured that out yet. I might head over to Florida, soak up some sun. I just need to recharge the batteries, y'know?"

"Of course. Go, have fun. Call me in a few days and let me know where you're at."

Collins saluted him. "No problem, Chief."

He turned on his heels and left the office, closing the door behind him. To the left of it was Kim Mitchell's desk. Jericho and Julie were nowhere to be seen. Kim was staring at her keyboard, typing away feverishly. She looked up as Collins passed and smiled.

"Everything okay, Ray?" she asked.

Collins smiled. He had always had a soft spot for her. She was in her early-fifties, divorced, no kids, with bottle-blonde hair that rested on her shoulders and a body most thirty-year-olds would kill for.

"All good, Miss Mitchell," he replied with a nod. "Don't suppose ya fancy a few days away in Florida, do ya?"

Kim's cheeks flushed red and she looked away, giggling. She took a lock of her hair between two fingers, twisting it around as she rested on her desk, pushing her keyboard away. She went to say something, but before she had chance, the door behind her opened. Buchanan's frame appeared in the doorway. He looked at them both in turn. Kim quickly composed herself and resumed her typing.

He shook his head and fixed Collins with a hard, semi-serious stare. "How many times do I have to tell you not to hit on my secretary?"

Collins saluted again. "One more time, apparently. I'm outta here, boss."

He walked along the hall and down the stairs at the end. Kim watched him go, and when she re-focused, she found Buchanan staring at her. He raised an eyebrow. "And *you* need to stop encouraging him."

They both smiled, and he disappeared back inside his office, closing the door quietly behind him.

2

A few hours later, Julie and Jericho were sitting on either side of the aisle on a Delta flight, bound for Montreal. The pilot had just announced they were due to land in the next half-hour. They had spent the first part of the journey in virtual silence. Any conversation they attempted to have was almost continually interrupted by passengers or flight attendants walking between them, so they resigned themselves to reading through the briefing on their client that Buchanan's secretary had prepared for them.

Julie loved flying and was always promising herself she would make more time to travel for leisure, although she hardly ever did. She accepted the fact her job afforded her the opportunity to see the world and felt content with that middle ground. She simply tried to make the most of the experience, despite the work.

She relaxed back in her seat, sipping the iced water she had ordered. She glanced sideways at Jericho, failing to suppress a smile as she watched him still struggling to get comfortable in the coach seats. His colossal frame used every millimeter of the seat, and his legs were bent so much that his knees were almost level with his shoulders.

He turned and saw her staring. His expression was deadpan as he rolled his eyes.

"I hate flying," he announced.

Julie burst out laughing, and after a moment, even Jericho had to smile.

He twisted in his seat, accidentally knocking the woman next to him with his elbow. He apologized before talking to Julie. "So, what do you think of this Hyatt guy?"

She shrugged. "Do you want my opinion based on what *was* written in the report or what wasn't?"

Jericho smiled. "Either."

"Well, it says he's worked for Caterham Financial Services for over fifteen years, as some kind of asset manager. Now I'm not an accountant, but I'm guessing you don't have your daughter kidnapped by a Mexican cartel if you're a boring, straight-as-an-arrow number-cruncher."

Jericho nodded. "Yeah, that's what I figured. Bottom line, I'm not judging. I haven't exactly been a boy scout in the past either. I just don't want any surprises when we get there, y'know?"

She glanced over at the passenger beside her, checking he still had his earphones in. Then she looked back at Jericho, leaned into the aisle and, in a low voice, said, "You mean like random gunfire and car crashes?"

He chuckled, matching her body language and tone. "Exactly."

"At the risk of jinxing it, I can't see us running into too much trouble. If he's conducting business, he's likely to be public and visible, which immediately reduces the risk of a threat. The Mexicans will undoubtedly know by now that their attempt at kidnapping and blackmail has failed, so they won't want to expose themselves by trying something else so soon. We just need to stick by his side until he's done whatever he's doing, and we're golden."

Jericho adjusted his position for the hundredth time, feeling unavoidable irritation that comfort still eluded him. "I hope you're right. Let's not forget, you were the one who said we wouldn't run into too much trouble on the trip to Mexico, and we all remember how that worked out."

Julie stuck her tongue out. "I'm just trying to remain optimistic. You should try it."

"It's hard to remain optimistic when you're being shot at. I'm a realist—it doesn't hurt as much."

"Whatever. You're just cranky because you can't fit in your seat."

She made a point of stretching her legs, letting out a low groan of comfort.

Jericho arched his brow. "That's just showing off. Anyway, I'm not cranky. Cranky is what kids are when they wake up for school. I'm pissed, to the point where I want to rip the wings off this goddamn plane just so we can land faster and I can get out of this stupid-ass seat."

Julie laughed, settled back in her seat, and closed her eyes. A few moments later, the pilot announced over the PA they were beginning their final approach. Jericho breathed a sigh of relief, knowing his discomfort was almost over.

They landed smoothly, taxiing to a stop twenty minutes later. As they only had one overnight bag each, they avoided the hour-long horror of baggage claim, instead sailing straight through Passport Control at Pierre Elliott Trudeau International Airport. They made their way to Arrivals, shuffling at a frustrating pace among the masses of people doing the same, and scanned the barrier near the exit. Julie nudged Jericho's arm and nodded toward a man holding a sign that said *GlobaTech Industries*. He wore a black suit with red trim and a matching hat. They exchanged a glance before heading over.

"We're with GlobaTech," announced Jericho, gesturing to the sign as they reached their chauffeur.

The man smiled courteously. "If you would follow me, please."

He turned and strode toward the doors. The pair of them followed. Jericho leaned close to Julie and whispered, "He'd better have a limo waiting for us. There's no way I'm sitting down for another half-hour with no leg room."

Julie shook her head. "Quit whining, you big baby."

Jericho shrugged. "I'm just saying..."

As they stepped outside, the cold wind hit them. They both shuddered involuntarily as the persistent, icy blast burrowed under their skin, gripping their nerve endings and reminding them a Canadian fall is a far cry from California's version.

It was late afternoon, and with daylight fading, a crimson hue had mixed with the gray clouds, creating a menacing yet picturesque backdrop for the Montreal skyline. The temperature was a severe departure from what they were used to, and neither of them had dressed for the change in climate. Julie wore a thin jacket, open, over a sleeveless top, with fitted jeans and knee-length brown boots. Jericho had a thin, white T-shirt stretched over his enormous frame, making it look smaller than it was. He wore dark jeans and work boots.

"Goddamn... it's freezing," he said.

Julie rolled her eyes. "Great, something else for you to moan about."

Jericho sighed. "Give me a break, would you? I just like

space and warmth, and so far, this trip has offered me neither."

"Really? You haven't mentioned it..."

Jericho smiled and fell silent. They followed the man across the short-stay parking lot toward a black stretch limousine. He stopped by the rear door and opened it ceremoniously. Jericho reached the car first but side-stepped, so Julie could climb in before him. He followed, and the driver shut the door behind them. Inside was spacious, with seats running almost the full length of both sides and a generous walkway between them.

Jericho sat with his back to the trunk. He leaned into the soft leather and stretched his legs out with a satisfying sigh. He slouched, resting his arms above his head and clasping his hands behind him.

"This is more like it," he said, smiling.

Julie had moved to the side, resting her feet on the seating opposite. "Finally! Maybe you'll shut up now?"

Jericho laughed. "Yeah, maybe."

Julie huffed and folded her arms. The driver climbed in behind the wheel, started the engine, and drove out of the parking lot. He made his way onto Route Transcanadienne and followed it for twenty kilometers, all the way into the business district of Montreal city. He navigated the steady stream of traffic with an expertise only honed through experience.

Julie moved beside Jericho and buzzed her tinted window down halfway, taking in the sights of a new city while keeping the unfriendly temperature at bay. Skyscrapers peaked and troughed against the clouds. Sidewalks bustled with the constant pulse of humanity. It was a busy city, but it felt like a different kind of busy from what she was used to.

The driver guided the limo to a stop in the parking bay outside a towering building. A moment later, the door closest to the curb opened. Julie climbed out, and Jericho shuffled across the seat, joining her a moment later.

The driver retrieved their bags from the trunk, handing each one to them in turn. "If you would please head inside and speak to the gentleman at the security desk, he will issue you with temporary passes that grant you access to the building. You will find Mr. Hyatt on the fourteenth floor."

"Thank you," said Julie.

The driver nodded once before returning to his car, pulling away and disappearing into the flow of traffic a minute later.

Jericho looked at her. "Shall we?"

She nodded. "Lead the way."

They walked side by side up the short flight of steps leading to the main entrance. Jericho pushed the door open, holding it for Julie before following her inside. The reception area resembled a high-class hotel more than an office. The front desk was in the center of the lobby. It was a circular enclosure, with a counter running waist-high all the way around. Computer stations were set up on the main compass points, with two women and two men visible, either talking on the phone or typing at the keyboard.

They approached one of the men, smiling professionally. They both reached into their pockets and pulled out their ID badges, flashing them as the man looked up.

"We're here to see Mr. Hyatt," explained Jericho. "He's expecting us."

The man nodded silently and fumbled on the desk in front of him, just out of sight. A moment later, he produced two security badges with VISITOR printed across them, inside plastic holders attached to green lanyards.

"You're required to wear these at all times while on the premises," he advised, handing them over. "Take the elevator to the fourteenth."

They each took one and placed it over their heads.

"Thanks," said Julie.

They walked across the polished, dark marble floor toward the bank of elevators lining the far wall.

"That welcome was colder than outside," observed Jericho.

"Yeah, I noticed that," agreed Julie. "I thought Canadians were meant to be friendly..."

They rode the elevator up to the fourteenth floor and stepped out into another foyer. The floor was covered in a thick maroon carpet, and there was a desk facing them. Short corridors stretched away on either side, into the main office area.

The woman behind the desk smiled at them politely. She was attractive in a subtle way, wearing minimal make-up to maximum effect. Her long, dark hair flowed down past her shoulders, and the jacket of a navy dress suit was visible behind the monitor in front of her.

"Can I help you?" she asked.

Jericho flashed her a smile. "We're here to see Mr. Hyatt. We have an appointment."

The secretary glanced down at her desk, checking the schedule she had beside her. After a moment, she looked back up at each of them, a flash of surprise on her face. "G-GlobaTech Industries?"

Julie nodded. "That's us."

The woman regained her composure and smiled again. "Follow me, please."

She stood, walked around the desk, and headed along

the corridor to her left. Jericho watched her. She was taller than he had imagined she would be, having a couple of inches on Julie. He noticed she wore long, thin heels, and the boost showed off her toned calves, just visible below the pencil skirt she wore. Her figure was slim, undoubtedly the product of an hour in the gym before and after work. Jericho cast an approving eye over her as they followed but snapped out of his trance when Julie punched his arm.

He turned to her and frowned. "What was that for?"

She pursed her lips and raised an eyebrow. "Oh, nothing. I just thought I was working with you, not Ray."

"Huh? What's that supposed to mean?"

"It means I thought *he* was the womanizing asshole."

He lowered his voice. "Just because I was checking her out, it doesn't mean anything. It's a perfectly natural thing to do. There's no harm in it, and most people would take it as a compliment."

Julie let out a short, impatient huff. "Whatever."

Jericho smiled. "Wait a second. Are you... are you *jealous*?" She shot him a look that made his smile instantly disappear and the hair on his arms stand up. He swallowed hard. "Okay, you're not jealous."

She shook her head with mild disbelief. "No, I'm not jealous, but good job at thinking so highly of yourself."

"So, what's wrong?"

"I'm a woman, Jericho, in case you hadn't noticed. I don't have to like someone to feel disrespected when they look at someone else in my company."

He nodded slowly. "Okay. I'm not gonna lie, Jules, that only *kinda* makes sense."

"Whatever," she said again.

Jericho fell silent, sensing it was best to let the conversation drop. In his limited experience with women, he knew that if he didn't understand what he had done wrong, it was usually better to stay quiet. It's too easy to inadvertently make things worse.

As they turned a corner at the end, the floor opened out into a large space filled with desks and muted conversations. Groups of people were separated by multicolored dividers, which also served to form walkways between workstations. Along the opposite wall were three offices. Two were modest in size, with a much larger one in the corner.

The secretary led them through the maze of desks toward the corner office. The door was closed, and the vertical blinds in the window beside it were shut.

She stopped outside, turning to face them and flashing a professional smile. "This is Mr. Hyatt's office. You can go right in."

"Thank you," said Julie. There was a hint of hostility in her voice, which the receptionist either didn't notice or was polite enough to ignore.

She moved to the door, knocked once as a courtesy, and walked inside. Jericho followed her, smiling his thanks to the secretary as he passed, who returned the gesture while holding his gaze a second longer than she needed to.

Hyatt was sitting behind his desk, his head buried in the paperwork strewn across the surface. He looked up as they entered, smiling hurriedly. "Thank you for coming." He gestured to the chairs opposite him. "Please, take a seat. I'll be right with you, I just need to run through these numbers quickly."

They both placed their bags beside the door and sat beside each other. Jericho waved his hand nonchalantly. "Take your time."

He looked around the office, familiarizing himself with

the surroundings. It was a breathtaking view. The windows ran floor-to-ceiling, almost the full width of the walls ahead of him and to the left, providing a panoramic glimpse of the city. The décor was simple, minimalistic. Hyatt's desk was made from a dark mahogany and mostly devoid of decoration. A picture frame with a flower in the corner was positioned on an angle to Hyatt's right and contained a photo of the girl they had rescued from Mexico a little over twenty-four hours ago.

Hyatt gathered the papers together in a neat pile and placed them in a tray to his left. He looked up at both of them. His eyes were bloodshot and sunken, and flecks of gray stubble covered his face and throat.

"I'm sorry about that," he said. "It was something urgent."

"It's fine," said Julie. "If it's convenient, we would like to discuss the terms of your protection with you prior to our detail starting in the morning."

He nodded. "Of course. Now I expect you to keep your distance during any meetings but stay close by when I'm on the move. No more than—"

Jericho held up a hand to silence him. He smiled apologetically. "Not *your* terms, Mr. Hyatt. Ours."

Hyatt frowned. "What do you mean?"

"We're very good at what we do," explained Julie. "You know that. But we're only as good as our clients allow us to be, which means if you want us to guarantee your safety, we need a few things from you."

"Such as?"

"Complete and total honesty," said Jericho. "We need to know exactly what's going on, so we can best prepare for anything that might threaten your safety."

"We also need unrestricted access to your schedule and

your staff," added Julie, "so we know the movements of you and the people you surround yourself with. Again, if we don't know everything, we can't prepare for everything, which potentially leaves you vulnerable."

"And while we're on the subject of your staff," said Jericho. 'You might want to think of something to explain why we're here. Your receptionist outside seemed surprised to see us. I imagine it's strange that an unassuming accountant would need personal security from a company such as ours."

Julie clicked her fingers and nodded. "That's a good point, Mr. Hyatt."

Hyatt sat back in his seat, momentarily thrown off-guard by the requests. He composed himself again, leaned forward, and rested his elbows on his desk. "I... I guess I could say you're evaluating me before coming on board as one of my clients."

Jericho shrugged. "Yeah, that could work. Maybe send something out to explain our presence over the next couple of days."

"I will," replied Hyatt. "Thank you. Now look, while it's a comfort to know you take your jobs so seriously, you must understand there are things I can't tell you. I have to abide by data protection laws. I can't just—"

"I understand," interrupted Jericho. "But you're also protected by those laws as part of your agreement with us, which means whatever you say goes no further. We're not here to cast judgment, and we're not obligated to liaise with any law enforcement agencies." He gestured quickly to himself and Julie. "We're both part of an elite team, a division of GlobaTech Industries specializing in... exceptional private security. Honestly, I don't care what you're involved in. My only concern is your safety. It's our responsibility to keep you alive and well, so we can get you back to your daughter. But I can't do that if I don't know what—or who—you need protecting from."

Hyatt flicked his gaze between the two of them, sensing from their unblinking, hard stares that he had no choice but to agree. He glanced away, sighing heavily. A moment later, he met their gaze again and nodded. "I have your word that whatever I say goes no further?"

"We risked our lives to save your daughter, Mr. Hyatt," said Julie. "We're prepared to do the same for you. What you do between nine and five isn't our concern."

He nodded again, satisfied he could trust them. "Okay, then. I manage the financial assets for people who simply want the most from their money. Investment brokers, property developers, you name it. They have a lot of capital, and it's my job to make sure they only pay the tax that's due and store their hard-earned dollars in the right kind of savings accounts, to garner the optimum level of interest—that kind of thing."

Jericho nodded. "Sounds straightforward."

"It is. But a few years ago, my wife filed for divorce, and despite the healthy percentage of commission I earn on these multi-million-dollar transactions, it wasn't nearly enough to keep her and the team of soul-sucking lawyers she hired satisfied. I have sole custody of my daughter, and I want to provide for her, like any father would. But my ex-wife wasn't making it easy for me, and I simply didn't have enough money. So, I... I began representing some less-than-reputable clients on the side."

Julie and Jericho exchanged a subtle glance, silently acknowledging their assumptions were correct.

"In the few years I've been doing it," he continued, "I've earned almost as much as this firm has paid me since the day I started, and I've never had any trouble. I pride myself on being open with my clients, and in return, they reward me with repeat business, recommendations, a generous cut, and protection."

"So, what happened this time?" asked Julie.

"Honestly? I have no idea. Neither does my client."

"And their name is...?" asked Jericho.

"Darius Silva," replied Hyatt after a moment's hesitation. "He's actually a nice guy, and we've become friends over the years. But there's no escaping what he does for a living, and he has enemies because of it. One of these enemies has discovered information about a specific transaction I'm overseeing for him. Something of great value to Mr. Silva. Presumably, they also know of my involvement. Knowing they can't get to Darius directly because of who he is, they apparently thought it worthwhile trying to get to me."

"So, that was why your daughter was taken..." observed Jericho.

He nodded. "Sadly, yes, and you will forever have my thanks for getting my darling Jessica back safely."

Jericho nodded back. "No problem. But it wasn't easy. When we got to Mexico, we were ambushed. Cartels make for powerful and dangerous enemies, Mr. Hyatt. We're not naïve enough to think their involvement is over."

"I know. I just..." He sighed. "This is all getting out of hand. I mean, *cartels*? How the hell did they get involved in all this?"

"You want my advice, Mr. Hyatt? Let us get someone in to scan your computer and your phone for bugs."

Hyatt's eyes widened. "You think I'm under some kind of

surveillance? That's crazy! This isn't a James Bond movie. People don't really do that kind of thing... do they?"

Jericho suppressed a smile. "Industrial espionage happens more often than you'd think, and wire-tapping is quite common. Plus, this isn't exactly all above board, is it? It's worth considering."

He held his hands up in resignation. "Okay, whatever you say. You're the experts here, I guess."

Julie nodded. "Correct. Now we'll need to know some details about this transaction everyone's so interested in."

Hyatt hesitated. "Erm... I'm not sure I'm comfortable with—"

"Mr. Hyatt, please," said Jericho, cutting him off before any excuses could be given. "We're not here for judgment or concerned with legalities, remember? Though it's worth mentioning that, given the nature of this particular client's business, those data protection laws you mentioned don't count for shit."

"We just need an idea of what we're dealing with," added Julie. "The more we know, the better we can protect you."

Hyatt looked around the room as he shifted in his seat, nervous and uncomfortable. Eventually, his gaze settled on Julie.

"I... It's..." He sighed. "There's a shipment arriving at the Port of Halifax in Nova Scotia in two days. I will need to be there to oversee the processing of it, to ensure it's handled, transferred, and shipped back out as it should be."

Julie and Jericho looked at each other, their minds immediately engaged, focusing on the next forty-eight hours.

"We need to see a layout of the port," said Julie. "Look at ways in and out. Docking lanes. Security levels."

Jericho nodded his agreement. "Buchanan will be able to get us what we need. We can work out attack and counterattack scenarios based on the location, should anything happen. We'll know every way someone could come at us, every way we can repel an attack, and every way we can get out of there in a hurry."

Julie looked back at Hyatt, noting his bemused and dumbfounded expression. "Don't worry, Mr. Hyatt. We will guarantee your safety while we're at the port. Once this shipment has been dealt with, how confident are you the threat to you and your family will be over?"

Hyatt shrugged. "I... ah... I don't know. But once the shipment leaves for its final destination, it will no longer be vulnerable. And by that, I mean it'll be too late for anyone to, y'know, steal it or whatever."

"You know that for sure?"

Hyatt nodded. "I know details about the shipment itself have leaked, but I can guarantee you no one knows where it's going after it leaves Halifax. I know it's heading to the Caymans eventually, but Mr. Silva has arranged a stop-off along the way that he's not even told me about. And he hasn't given me a reason for it. Maybe he's extra paranoid, I don't know. Whatever the reason, I'm hoping once whoever is behind all this realizes that, they won't come after me again."

Jericho got to his feet. Julie did the same a moment later.

"Okay," he said to Hyatt. "We have a few calls to make and some things to prepare." He checked his watch. "It's getting late. You should finish for the day and go to a hotel until this is over. Make it somewhere public."

"Won't that make me easier to find?"

Jericho shook his head. "It will make you harder to get to. Staying public, where the whole world can see you, is much safer than hiding away. Your driver was a nice guy. Get him to run you there and then have him contact us with the name of the hotel and your room number. We'll get rooms there and come get you at five a.m. tomorrow. Once we do, we won't leave your side until this is all over."

Hyatt nodded. "Sure, okay. Whatever you say."

Jericho and Julie took turns to shake his hand before heading for the door, collecting their bags as they passed. Julie glanced over her shoulder. "Don't worry, Mr. Hyatt. We'll keep you safe, and we'll have you back with your daughter soon, I promise."

They left and made their way out of the building. The sun had sunk even lower in the time they had spent with Hyatt, and daylight was almost nothing but a memory. Traffic was still heavy, and the glow of headlights dominated the streets.

"I'll put in a call to Buchanan," said Julie, taking her cell from her pocket. "We should let him know exactly what he's signed us up for and what we need."

Jericho nodded and paced away to the edge of the sidewalk, twisting his body to slide between the steady stream of pedestrians. He looked both ways along the street, scanning the city with an expert eye for anything that seemed out of place. No one stood out. There were no parked cars with people inside. Yet, despite it looking as if the world was business as usual, he couldn't shake the growing feeling in his gut that something wasn't right. He believed every word Hyatt had said to them but worried his naivety would lead to him underestimating the severity of what he was facing. A large-scale drug operation. Illegal cash. Rival gangs. He sighed, fully aware of how quickly things could take a turn for the worst.

He glanced back at Julie, who was still speaking to their

boss on the phone. Between them, he was sure they could handle anything, regardless of his own concerns. He nodded to himself as he took one last look along the street and muttered, "Time to go to work."

3

The sea of bodies shuffled like the constant motion of the tide as people desperately fought for some personal space in the uncomfortable warmth of the sports bar. The evening was in full swing. A large screen mounted on the wall facing the entrance showed a live baseball game, but the commentary was barely audible over the chatter from the crowd.

Julie and Jericho stood side by side at a waist-high, circular table close to the bar counter, nursing half-empty bottles of beer. The stools had been taken by other customers, no doubt squeezed into a space too small around another table.

After leaving Hyatt's office, they had traveled to the GlobaTech site in the city—their equivalent of a field office —to arm themselves. They were unable to bring their own weapons with them across the border, so getting new ones was a priority before their security detail began. Buchanan had sent the information they requested about the port there too, so it was waiting for them when they arrived. They spent time on their strategy, working with a security team on site to familiarize themselves with the layout and to prepare for every eventuality they could think of.

Once they were happy with their preparations, they had called Hyatt's secretary, who put them in touch with his driver. He advised them which hotel he had taken Hyatt to, so they headed straight there and checked in to single rooms one floor below their client. They both grabbed showers and a change of clothes before heading out for a bite to eat. There was an inexpensive steakhouse a few blocks from where they were staying, and they ate with the experienced enthusiasm of soldiers who understand their next meal might not be for a while.

Before turning in for the evening, they decided to get a couple of drinks, relax, and soak up a little of the local atmosphere. A lot of what they did relied on instinct, and it helped to have a good understanding of the environment.

The sports bar was only one block over from the restaurant, and when they arrived, it hadn't looked too busy. However, a half-hour later, once the baseball game had started, the place was bulging at the seams.

Jericho felt claustrophobic, yet again confined to a space not suited to his huge frame. He struggled to lift his arm as he drank and shifted his weight restlessly back and forth on each leg in an effort to find a comfortable position.

He leaned forward, turning to his colleague. "I'm sorry about before, Jules."

She was staring blankly at the surface of the table but looked at him as he spoke, frowning. "For what?"

"You know... for everything at Hyatt's office. With the secretary..."

She smiled, waving a hand dismissively before returning her gaze to the table. "Forget about it. I was being silly."

He shook his head slightly to himself, momentarily

stunned by her apparent change in attitude. He never pretended to understand what went on inside a woman's head, but he wasn't about to question it.

He nodded. "Okay, it's forgotten. So, how are you feeling about tomorrow?"

She shrugged. "Normal, I guess. It's a job like any other, right? I mentioned your concern about gaps in Hyatt's security and potential surveillance to Buchanan. He's going to send a couple of guys over tomorrow to give the entire floor of Hyatt's office building a once-over. Same with his hotel room."

"I think that's a smart move. His client's enemies found out about his business, his daughter, and us. If he has a leak, I'd rather we plug it before we step between him and any flying bullets."

Julie nodded. "I agree. As for Hyatt, I feel better now that I've seen the layout for the docks. I reckon he's safe for now. It'll be when the money's being loaded onto the ship that we'll struggle."

"Yeah, I was thinking the same thing. At least we only need worry about *him*. His client and their people can worry about everything else."

Julie slammed her palm down on the table and gestured to the large screen with her bottle. "Oh, come on! He wasn't out! Who's that official? Stevie Wonder?"

Jericho laughed with disbelief. "Since when are you a baseball fan?"

She smiled. "Since always. I've got my three older brothers to thank for it. They used to take me to games when I was young. I got a passion for it early on in life, and it's stayed with me."

Jericho took a swig from his bottle. "Well, I never knew that about you."

She winked. "I could write a book on the things you don't know about me, big guy."

They smiled, holding each other's gaze for a moment before taking another sip of their drinks. A loud cheer erupted through the bar, and they both looked over at the screen to see the replay of a home run.

"Who's, ah... who's playing anyway?" asked Jericho.

Julie looked at him and smiled. "Now I *know* you don't care!"

He shrugged. "Just... showing an interest, that's all."

"Okay. The Blue Jays are hosting the Braves. They're up four-nothing, and that was their third homer of the game. It's bottom of the fourth, and the local boys are looking good."

Jericho emptied his bottle and smiled. "That's... wow, that's great. Gotta love them homers, am I right?"

Julie stared at him, her lip curled in bemusement. "You didn't understand a word I just said, did you?"

"Well, I... I mean, obviously..." Jericho sighed. "No, I didn't. You might as well have been speaking Japanese."

Julie laughed, reached up, and patted him playfully on the cheek. "Never mind, big guy."

"Hey, don't pity me, woman! I was a military brat. I spent my youth traveling the world, learning how to fight. I didn't have time to watch grown men play catch in their pajamas, all right?"

She chuckled again. "Okay, you keep telling yourself that."

A waitress approached the table, carrying a large tray half-covered with empties precariously in one hand. She was young, attractive, small in stature, and looked very tired. Jericho noted the size of the tray and thought how impressive it was she could carry it one-handed while navigating the huge crowd.

"Can I get you folks another round?" she asked, collecting their bottles.

"I'll have a beer, thanks," said Julie before gesturing to Jericho with her thumb. "And get my lady friend here a white wine spritzer, with one of those little umbrellas in it, would you?"

Jericho rolled his eyes at her before smiling apologetically at the waitress. "Forgive my colleague. She can't handle her drink. After one bottle, she thinks she's a stand-up comedian. I'll just have a beer. Thanks."

The waitress laughed. "Coming right up."

Jericho made way for her to pass, then turned to Julie. "Very funny."

She stuck her tongue out. "Well, that's what you get."

"For what?"

"For—"

Before she could answer, there was a loud noise behind them. They both looked around to see the waitress knelt down, surrounded by half a tray's worth of broken glass that was scattered across the floor. Just to the side of her, three guys were standing in a line. One of them had a large wet patch on his leg, and the other two were laughing.

The one with the wet leg leaned forward, bending over to speak to the waitress. "Watch where you're going, you stupid bitch!"

Still crouching, the waitress looked up at the man, tears welling in her eyes. "I'm... I'm *really* sorry. I didn't mean to—"

"I don't care what you didn't mean to do," he continued, pointing to his leg. "These are expensive pants, and you've just ruined them."

She stood and took a small step away, holding her hands out. "I'm sorry. I... I didn't see you. Let me get you—"

"Get me what? A free drink? Not good enough! You owe me a new pair of pants. These were a hundred and ten dollars. I bet you can't even afford that on your crappy wage, can you?"

Despite the lack of room, the crowd had moved to give the scene a wide berth, leaving the waitress and the three men in a spacious circle. The loud rabble of conversation had stopped, and only the commentary coming from the TV broke the silence. No one said anything, apart from a few whispers. Most just stood watching, while a few fumbled in their pockets for their cell phone, undoubtedly wanting to document the drama for social media.

"I'll tell you what," said the man. "How about you make it up to me another way?"

The waitress frowned. "W-what do you mean?"

"I mean, how's about we head out back, and you can get me out of these pants... give them a rub dry for me?"

He turned to look at his two friends, who were still laughing.

The waitress took another step back. "I... I'm sorry about your drink, okay? Let me get you another one, on the house."

The man took a step forward and grabbed her wrist. "What did I just say, bitch?"

Jericho took a deep breath, sensing the rush of anger erupting inside of him. He flexed his shoulders and tensed every inch of his body, fighting to control the flash of fury. He looked on, giving the man every opportunity to let go of the waitress, to back down and apologize.

But he didn't.

Beside him, Julie noticed the sudden change in his body

language and, knowing from experience exactly what it meant, placed her hand on his arm. "Jericho, don't get involved."

He ignored her, staring intently at the scene, his jaw muscles clenching repeatedly.

The man started to drag the waitress toward him, pulling her over the broken glass. She screamed, struggling against his grip to get free, but it was futile.

"Let go of me!" she yelled.

The man's friends had stopped laughing, instead turning their attention to the crowd of onlookers, staring challengingly at the two male bar staff who had come to see what was happening.

"Come on, bitch," replied the man as he pulled her toward him. "Quit playing hard to get. You owe me!"

Julie watched for a moment before letting go of Jericho's arm and gesturing exasperatedly. "Y'know what? Knock yourself out. That asshole deserves it."

Without a word, Jericho stood, cracked his neck and strode with bad intentions toward the scene. Julie looked on and let out a heavy sigh, knowing all too well what was about to happen.

"I gave you every chance..." she muttered.

Jericho stepped into the circle, and the man snapped his head left to stare at him, wavering momentarily as he processed the size of him. Then he glanced over his shoulder at his friends, who instinctively moved to his side. He looked back at Jericho, laughing.

"This ain't nothing to do with you, asshole," he said. "Walk away."

Jericho shrugged. "Let her go, and I will."

The man frowned. "Who are you, her granddaddy? Get the hell out of here before you get hurt."

Julie placed her head in her hand.

"Ah, crap. Why did you have to go and say something stupid?" she said to herself, frustrated by the man's apparent lack of intelligence.

"Last warning," continued Jericho, taking a small step toward the men. "Let... her... go."

The man held his gaze for a few tense moments before shoving the waitress to the floor. "Whatever, asshole. She should've been more careful. Besides, I was just having a little fun. I guess now I'll have to have some fun with you."

Julie pushed her way into the circle, ignoring everyone there, and headed straight for the waitress. She leaned forward and helped her to her feet.

"What's your name, sweetie?" she asked.

The waitress sniffed back tears. "Evie."

"Okay, Evie, you're gonna want to come with me."

"W-why? What's going to happen?"

Julie walked her back over to their table, making brief eye contact with Jericho as they passed. Once they were safely away from the scene, she replied, "Those douchebags are about to have a very bad night, and you don't wanna get caught in the middle of it. Trust me."

Jericho's unblinking gaze stayed transfixed on the man and his friends. In his peripheral vision, he saw Julie move the waitress out of harm's way. He took another step forward, moving to the center of the circle, ignoring the shards of glass that crunched underfoot.

The man looked at his friends and laughed as he gestured at Jericho. "Who does this guy think he is? I bet he just wants that piece of ass for himself!"

Jericho stared at him. "I'm the man you think you are. Now you owe that young woman an apology, and you're not leaving until she gets one."

The man scoffed. "Is that right? Well, listen, tough guy, the way I see it, she should be apologizing to *me*. I'm the one with a wet leg."

"Better wet than broken."

"What did you say?"

"You heard me."

The man chuckled. "No, I don't think I did. Say it again for me and my friends here because it sounded like a threat. Are you *threatening* me, asshole?"

Jericho took a deep, impatient breath. "Okay, look. Clearly, I'm talking to an idiot. I didn't realize, and that's on me, so I tell you what I'll do. I'll speak a little slower and use smaller words that you'll understand, all right?"

The man clenched his fists, seething through his gritted teeth.

Jericho continued. "You need to say sorry to that young woman for hurting her. You do that, and maybe you don't end up like all this glass..."

He shook his head, his anger giving way to confusion. "What does that even mean?"

"...spread across the floor in pieces."

"Would you listen to yourself? There are three of us, man. And you think *I'm* an idiot?"

"Yeah, I do. I'm also surprised you can count to three."

The man's expression changed again, from confusion to impatience. He glared through wide eyes, breathing hard. "You think you're funny? Let's see how funny you are when you're dead, asshole!"

He reached behind him and produced a switchblade. The blade was clean, thin, maybe seven inches long. His friends postured up on either side of him, as if drawing confidence from the weapon.

Jericho looked at each of them in turn. They all

appeared to be capable guys—on the surface, at least. They were smaller than him but still big men. All at least six foot, all maybe weighing around two-twenty. None of them were star athletes, but they each packed more muscle than fat. Given how they had been acting so far, he figured they were no strangers to bar fights. Probably no strangers to winning them either. But they were amateurs at best. The guy with the knife was holding it as if he were using it to eat a meal.

Jericho thought back to his military training. He was always told if someone pulled a blade during a fight, don't worry about it if you can see it. If they're waving it around, trying to look intimidating, it's too easy to take it off them. They simply don't know what they're doing. The dangerous people are the ones who hide it, usually by gripping the handle and holding the knife upside-down, so the blade is pressed against the inside of the forearm. You wouldn't see it coming until it was sticking out of you.

Jericho stood his ground, silently inviting them to make a move. He knew he couldn't instigate anything, but he wasn't going to back down now. The waitress wasn't about to get a voluntary apology, which meant the situation was only going to end one way.

The man with the knife snarled, took a step toward him, and lunged the blade forward violently. Jericho had a considerable reach advantage and threw a straight right fist with deadly precision. It connected with the man's nose, causing it to break and bleed long before the knife could pose a problem. His eyes watered, and Jericho quickly grabbed his wrist, twisting it counter-clockwise, forcing the man to drop the knife. He slid it away behind him with his foot and threw another strong punch to the guy's sternum. It knocked the air from his lungs and sent him crashing to the floor.

He took a step back, anticipating retaliation from one of the remaining two men. He figured one of them would be smart enough to know a lost cause when they saw one, but it would probably take one more body to convince him.

It was the one to his left who made the move.

He came forward quickly, winding up a haymaker that Jericho telegraphed with ease. He side-stepped, allowing the man's own momentum to carry him forward. As he drew level, Jericho snapped his torso clockwise, delivering an elbow to the man's jaw. The impact was dull and heavy, and he felt bone give way beneath it. The man dropped like a stone, landing face-first on the glass. Jericho glanced down and saw his cheek had been shattered.

He looked at the last man, who was rooted to the spot, eyes were wide with fear and sweat beaded on his brow.

"Why don't you speak on behalf of your friends?" asked Jericho, gesturing over to his table, where the waitress was looking on, dumbfounded.

The remaining guy nodded hurriedly and looked over at her. "S-s-sorry, lady."

Jericho smiled. "There. That wasn't too bad, was it?" He pointed at the two men on the floor. "Now get these sorry sonsofbitches outta here. They're making the place look untidy."

He moved quickly to his friends but, seeing they were both unconscious, left them where they were and bolted for the exit.

Jericho walked back to his table, taking an exaggerated step over the men on the floor. Julie regarded him. "You feel better now?"

He nodded. "I always do after doing the right thing." He looked at the waitress. "You all right?"

She nodded, rubbing her wrist. "I'm fine. Thank you.

But you really didn't have to do that. We get jerks like that in here all the time. You get used to it, y'know?"

Julie placed a hand on her arm. "Sweetie, that's not something you should *ever* have to get used to. Hopefully, my friend has deterred anyone else from thinking about putting their hands on you."

Evie smiled at them both in turn before making her way back over to the bar. The crowd closed the circle again, and everyone turned their attention back to the big screen.

Jericho leaned forward, resting his crossed arms on the table. Julie did the same beside him. After a few minutes of silence, she said, "So, you wanna call it a night? Or would you like to break a few more faces before bedtime?"

Jericho looked over at her and smiled. "No, I'm good."

She stood to her full height, which was still smaller than Jericho, despite him leaning over. "Come on, you gigantic, hot-tempered, lovable gentleman. We've got an early start in the morning."

He nodded, stood up, and held his arm out for her to link. She took it with a smile, and the two of them headed for the door. The crowd parted respectfully for them, and they were soon outside, appreciating the evening's cold temperature for the first time since they arrived.

Julie lay on her bed, staring at the solitary crack in the ceiling. There was almost total silence in the spacious room. She was high enough in the building that any noise from the street below was minimal at best. She could hear Jericho snoring in the next room, but that wasn't why she was still awake. She glanced at the clock on the bedside table next to her. It was turned two a.m. She sighed and rolled over on her front, burying her face in the pillow. She was wide-eyed and alert, her brain still wired, thinking about the new detail she would be starting in a few hours. It was the same every time.

She pushed herself up and reached for her phone, which was plugged in beside her, charging. She sat on the bed, her legs crossed, and selected a contact from her list to begin dialing. It rang out. Ten seconds. Fifteen. She was about to give up and then it was answered.

"Hello?"

She smiled. "Hey... Dad, it's me. Did I wake you?"

"Julie? It's one in the morning—of course, you woke me. Is everything all right?"

His voice was whiskey-rough and a little disoriented, but she grinned regardless, seeking comfort in his gravelly tone. "Yeah, everything's fine. It's two a.m. here, actually. I'm sorry. I know it's late."

Her father coughed away from the phone, his breathing raspy and momentarily hindered. "Nah, I don't give a damn about the time. You know me. I don't sleep much anyway. Where are you, sunflower?"

Julie's smile faded, her lips forming a tight, crooked line as she fought back a tear. Ever since she was a child, she had always been his *sunflower*, and even now, with her fortieth birthday on the horizon, he still insisted on using that name.

"I'm in Montreal," she said, sniffing back her emotion. "I'll be here for a few days with work."

There was a pause. "Are you okay? Are you safe?"

"Yeah, everything's fine. It's just a standard protection gig. Nothing to worry about."

"You're still working for GlobaTech, then?"

She nodded, despite herself. "I am."

"Ah, I don't know why you went back to those people. After what they did to you and your friends after Prague..."

"That was unavoidable. You know that as well as I do, Dad. But they're the good guys. The world needs more people like GlobaTech, and I'm honored to be a part of it. It's fine, I promise."

Her father scoffed playfully. "Who am I kidding? You won't listen to me anyway. You're stubborn, just like your mother was."

A single tear escaped, trickling down her cheek and splashing onto her top. She knew he wasn't being awkward or vindictive. His tone always softened when he mentioned her mother, as if speaking about her triggered a fond memory.

"You wouldn't have it any other way," she said, laughing.

"You got that right, sweetheart."

"So, how are you? Are the nurses treating you okay?"

"Oh, never mind about me. You don't wanna hear all about an old man. Tell me what's going on with you."

"Dad, please... I called you because I was thinking about you. I couldn't sleep, and my mind was racing, y'know? I thought of you, and... I just wanted to check in."

He sighed. "Well, it's nice to know you're thinking of me, I guess. I'm okay, sweetheart. This place is... it's all right. I'm not too keen on the woman who gives me sponge baths though."

Julie chuckled. "Why?"

"She's too rough. Too heavy-handed. She's a big lady, if you catch my drift. When she's done, I feel violated, not clean."

She burst out laughing, catching her voice almost instantly, aware of the time. "Dad!"

"What? I'm just saying... you pay eighteen hundred dollars a month for care, you expect a little TLC, that's all."

She lay back on the bed, stretched her legs out, and sighed a relaxing sigh. "Thanks, Dad."

"For what?"

"For not being mad that I called you so late. And for being you."

"Well, who else am I gonna be?"

She rolled her eyes, sensing the moment was lost on him. "I'll let you get some sleep. When I'm finished here, I'm gonna come see you, okay?"

He coughed again. "That'd be lovely."

"Night, Dad."

"I love you, sunflower."

"I love you too."

She hung up, tossed the phone to the end of the bed, and shuffled up so that her head sank back into the pillow. Within minutes, she was asleep, a slight smile on her face.

4

_____

Jericho stepped out of the shower, drying himself quickly with a towel before padding naked across his room to his travel bag. He took out underwear, socks, and a shoulder holster, placing them on the bed. He moved to the mirror mounted on the wall opposite and checked his reflection. He ran a hand over his head, feeling the short, coarse hair grate on his palm. Then he stroked his chin and throat. He needed a shave, but it was still short enough to get away with calling it 'designer' stubble, so it could wait another day.

He got dressed, grimacing to himself when he fastened the top button of his shirt, feeling it tight against his throat. He hated suits and ties. He found them too restricting, but they were a necessary evil when it came to security details. He fastened his tie and slid his holster on over his arms, adjusting the straps to ensure it was tight against the left side of his chest. He clipped the comms unit to the back of his belt and fed the wire up and over his shoulder, securing the earpiece in place.

He walked back over to his bed and reached under his pillow, retrieving the GlobaTech handgun he had collected the previous day. It was nicknamed *The Negotiator*. Jericho had been involved in the testing of the weapon when it first came out of development a couple of years ago. Now it was standard-issue. He checked the mag and chambered a round. He placed his thumb on the scanner built into the butt, checking it turned blue and recognized his print. Happy it was in working order, he holstered it and shrugged his jacket on. He paused for a moment to check his reflection one last time and make sure he was smart and presentable. Finally, he picked up his watch from the nightstand and fastened it around his wrist, checking the time before covering it with his sleeve.

Four-thirty-two a.m.

He rolled his eyes and left the room, turning right and stopping at the next door along. He raised his hand to knock, but as he did, the door opened. Julie was standing there, dressed in a smart, fitted trouser suit. Her auburn hair was tied back in a ponytail, and he could see her earpiece.

She looked him up and down, smiling. "James Bond, eat your heart out."

Jericho remained deadpan. "Be quiet."

"Oh, lighten up. Are you *still* not used to early starts?"

He stepped back, allowing her out of her room. "I just like my sleep, that's all."

She shut the door before turning to look at him. "So, you need comfort, warmth, and now sleep to stop being a moody asshole? The list of things that stop you complaining is growing by the day."

"What? I'm just saying..."

She rolled her eyes. "Yeah, I know."

They set off walking along the hall, to the elevator at the end. "Anyway, at least you got *some* sleep," she continued. "I could hear you snoring."

He raised both eyebrows with surprise. "Really?"

"Yeah, I couldn't switch off, and I heard you through the walls."

"Now that you mention it, I thought I heard *you* laughing last night..."

She smiled fondly. "Yeah, I gave my dad a call."

"Ah, how is he?"

She shrugged. "He seems okay."

"Is that care home looking after him?"

She chuckled. "Yeah, despite the rough sponge baths, apparently."

Jericho smiled. "Do I wanna know?"

"Nah, he was just complaining. You two have a lot in common, actually—you both complain all the time. Difference is, he *is* an old man, whereas you just sound like one!"

Jericho laughed. "Well, at least you refrained from an easy age joke..."

They reached the elevator, and Julie pressed the call button. "Are you kidding me? After what you did to that guy last night when he called you 'granddaddy'? No way am I having a pop at your age again."

They smiled together as the doors opened in front of them with a ding. They stepped inside, and Jericho pushed the button for the next floor up. A few moments later, they were walking along the hall toward Hyatt's suite. They paused outside his room.

"We're early," said Julie. "We said five, and it's only four-forty."

"It'll be fine. No way a man in his position is sleeping much."

Jericho knocked on the door. They waited a few moments, but there was no answer from inside. He frowned and knocked again. "Mr. Hyatt, it's Stone and Fisher from GlobaTech."

Still nothing.

The two of them exchanged a glance, noting each other's expressions change, their jaws clenching with concern.

"Mr. Hyatt?" tried Julie. "Can you let us in, please?"

Silence.

She turned to Jericho. "You don't think he's...?"

He frowned. "What? Been taken?"

"Or worse."

"Well, I do *now*." He let out a taut breath. "That's it."

Julie stepped away as he backed up to the opposite wall. He took a deep breath to compose himself and then paced forward, letting out a low, guttural roar through gritted teeth as he thrust his leg forward, slamming his foot into the door, just above the handle.

It whipped open, hitting the inside wall with a loud bang and detaching from the hinges at the top. Julie strode in, drawing her own *Negotiator* and crouching low. She paused in the doorway to the bathroom on the right, holding her gun low, covering the angle. Jericho followed, drawing his own weapon and leaning high against the opposite wall, covering the room.

It was dark inside as sunrise was still a couple of hours away. The room was far bigger than either his or Julie's. He could barely make out the shape of the bed a short way in front of him.

Julie moved level, nodded once, and then spun around the corner, dropping low again. As she did, the light flicked on, and the room was bathed in a bright, artificial glow, which stunned the pair of them. Squinting as they stared briefly at the floor, waiting for their eyes to adjust, they heard a voice say, "What the hell is going on?"

They both looked over to see Ulysses Hyatt sitting upright in bed, one hand still on the light switch beside him, the other nervously clutching a small baseball bat.

They holstered their weapons, letting out sighs of relief. Julie turned to Jericho and patted him on the shoulder. "Swing and a miss, big guy... swing and a miss."

She walked out of the room without a word. Jericho looked at Hyatt, absently scratching the back of his head. "Sorry about the door. Ah... when you didn't answer, we thought... and then we..." He sighed. "I'll be outside."

Forty minutes later, the three of them left the hotel, with Julie and Jericho flanking Hyatt on either side. His car was waiting for them at the back of the hotel, with the driver standing by the open rear door.

"Good morning, sir," he said courteously as they approached.

Hyatt nodded a silent greeting before ducking inside the limousine. The driver looked at Julie. "How are you today, madam?"

She smiled. "Madam? Uh-uh. If we're going to be around for a few days, you can call me Julie, okay?"

The driver nodded. "As you wish."

"And I'm fine, thank you. We're going straight to the office."

He nodded again, and she climbed inside, moving to one of the seats lining the side of the vehicle. Jericho climbed in last, sitting beside Hyatt. The door closed behind him, and a moment later, the engine turned over and they set off.

5

The blonde woman stepped out of the shower, dripping water on the tiled floor. Not bothering to dry herself or even cover up, she walked out of the bathroom, across the plush, cream carpet of the hotel room, and through the sliding doors that led out onto the balcony.

Ray Collins was leaning on the railing, looking down at the swimming pool. The sun was still climbing in the pale morning sky, and the temperature was rising quickly. The pool area was already packed with gorgeous women and muscular men.

With the exception of his Aviator sunglasses, he was also completely naked. A cigarette dangled loosely between his fingers. He felt wet arms snake around his waist, squeezing gently as the bare breasts of his fair-haired companion pressed against his back.

"Hey, darlin'. Nice shower?"

"Oh, Ray, this place is amazing!"

He turned to face her and smiled. "It's a crime ya've never been to Miami before."

The blonde nodded in agreement. "I know! And I've never stayed in a hotel as nice as *this*!"

He took a long drag on the cigarette, turning his head to the side as he blew a thin plume of blue-gray smoke into the air, trying his best to remember the girl's name.

Yes, she was half his age, and no, he didn't care.

He put the cigarette out on the balcony railing and flicked the stub over the side, turning to face the young blonde. He eyed her up and down approvingly. *Stunning* didn't even come close. She was a lingerie model, and they had met the night before, shortly after his arrival in Miami. He rented a car at the airport when he landed and drove to the hotel. He checked in, grabbed a quick shower, and headed straight back out to the nearest bar. Within an hour, he had found himself talking to...

"*Alyana*," he said, smiling as her name came back to him, "why don't ya get yourself a drink from the minibar? I'll be right in."

He knew his accent drove her wild. She giggled and threw her arms around his neck, standing on her tiptoes to kiss him before disappearing inside. He watched her go and then resumed leaning on the balcony, looking down at the crowded pool area. He was content taking his time. He knew what was waiting for him inside, and he knew it wouldn't last forever. He appreciated the break, but he always missed the job. He took a deep breath, savoring the warmth before walking back inside the apartment.

Alyana was pouring them both a drink. He noticed the row of empty spirit bottles lined on the tabletop in front of her.

That's gonna cost me, he thought.

She turned as he entered and came running over to him, still wet, still naked. She placed her arms around his neck and kissed him before he could say a word. He placed his hands on her waist, lifting her up with ease. She wrapped her shapely legs around him, and he carried her over to the bed. They fell playfully onto the mattress, locked in their embrace and oblivious to the world.

He felt her hands on the back of his head, pulling him toward her. He leaned down to kiss her soft, full lips. Collins was truly lost in the moment, but a familiar noise dragged him back to a far less exciting reality.

His lips still pressing against hers, he tilted his head slightly and glanced at his cell phone on the bedside table, moving closer to the edge as it vibrated.

He went to move for it, but Alyana stopped him. "Just leave it, baby. Stay with me..."

She tried to kiss him again, but his curiosity needed satisfying before anything else. He grabbed the phone and looked at the caller ID. It was a withheld number.

"Ah, screw it," he muttered.

He declined the call and placed the phone back on the table. He shuffled back and resumed his position beside the young woman.

"I'm sorry, love. I thought it might be work. Now, where were we?"

An hour passed by in a heartbeat. Alyana had fallen asleep, resting on his chest. The thin, silk bedsheet was draped over her waist, shaping itself to her legs and curves. Collins lay awake, staring at the ceiling, replaying the last twenty-four hours over and over in his head. Every kiss, every touch, every drink...

He felt restless—guilty, almost, for leaving his team-mates to take on another job while he went on vacation. They all had it rough in Mexico. What made him so special?

He let out a relaxed sigh, trying to work out if he really needed any downtime at all.

Alyana stirred beside him, turning her body and rolling off him, which he took as a sign and gently climbed out of bed, careful not to disturb her. He quickly threw his clothes on, which consisted of knee-length denim shorts, white sneakers, and a thin Hawaiian shirt that he wore with the top two buttons unfastened. He grabbed his cell phone, cigarettes, and sunglasses and headed for the door.

"Where are you going?" asked Alyana drowsily.

Collins looked back over his shoulder. "I think I'm done with Miami, baby. But listen—the room's paid up for the week, so why don't ya relax and enjoy yaself? I'll call ya, okay?"

She didn't look happy, but she smiled. "Okay. I... I love you..."

Collins didn't skip a beat. "Heh... and who can blame ya, honey?"

He winked at her before putting his shades on and walking out into the hall. As he closed the door, he heard her shout, "Wait... you don't have my number!"

He smiled to himself as he walked along the hall to the elevator. He rode it down to the lobby and made his way outside, pausing briefly to wink at the attractive brunette behind the front desk, who was staring at him with a playful smile on her face.

He strolled over to his rental car—a white convertible with the top down. Luckily, he had parked in what little shade there was. As he put one hand on the door, he froze. He felt an unmistakable cold pressure against the back of his skull. Immediately, his mind was engaged, thinking about all the possible things that could have happened that led to him having a gun to his head and all the things that could conceivably happen from that moment onward.

"Nice and easy," said a deep, Hispanic voice behind him.

Collins half-turned but didn't need to look to see who it was. He recognized the voice, and his shoulders slumped forward slightly with resignation and dread. He let out a loud and exaggerated breath. "Victor, ya podgy bastard... how've ya been?"

"Flattery will get you nowhere, you stupid... Leprechaun... prick!"

He slowly moved to face the man, making sure he allowed the gun barrel to stay touching his head. The man he knew as Victor was wearing a dark gray suit, jacket open, and a white shirt. He was overweight, and his clothes fought to stay fastened over his frame. Sweat patches marked his chest and collar.

Collins chuckled at the inadequacy of the man's retort. "What d'ya want, Victor?"

"The same thing I wanted the last couple of times I paid you a visit," replied Victor, wheezing slightly in the heat. "Our money."

"And like I told ya last time, ya'll get it."

He held his hands out to the side as Victor moved his gun close to his body, concealing it from passers-by. Collins looked him up and down. "Seriously, man, how the hell are ya dressed like *that* in Miami?"

"You're in no position to offer fashion advice," countered Victor. He took a deep breath and pushed his large stomach out a little more, further stretching the buttons on his shirt. "Now you owe my employer fifty large. You've owed it for quite some time, and if you couldn't pay it back before, you definitely can't afford it with all the interest. You're out of second chances, Ray."

Collins casually glanced around, checking to see if Victor had any friends close by. He couldn't see any. He took his sunglasses off, folded them up, and put them in the breast pocket of his shirt.

"All right, look. Ya've caught me at a bad time, Vic. I'm just heading home after some vacation time, and I'm a little light on funds right now. Give me a couple of days to get back, speak to my bank, gather the money. I'll give ya my address, ya can come 'round to mine, I'll pay ya back, we can have a few tequilas... it'll be just like old times. Whaddaya say?"

Victor waved the barrel of his gun in an effort to draw Collins' attention to it. "We're doing this now."

"I don't have the money, Vic. Were ya not listening just then? I'm good for it, but I don't have it on me this second."

"Then I take the car, for collateral. And I break your thumbs, for pleasure." He smiled a big, greasy smile, his large jowls wobbling as he chuckled. "On top of the fifty Gs."

Collins shrugged. "The car's a rental, so be my guest. But as for the thumbs, let's be honest here, Vic. The only way ya'd break anything of mine is if ya fell on me.'

Victor's smile disappeared, and he took a step back, raising his weapon high and taking a slow, deliberate aim at Collins' head.

"Hey, hey, hey—take it easy, *Jabba*," said Collins, instinctively conscious of any collateral damage. People around them had taken notice, and screams sounded out as they saw the gun. "Just gimme a second here, and I'm sure we can—"

He stopped talking as he whipped his hand up, grabbing Victor's wrist and lifting it skyward, so the gun wasn't pointing at anyone. With an open palm, he jabbed the curved inside edge of his hand, between the thumb and the index finger, hard into Victor's throat. The overweight debt collector gasped for breath as his eyes went wide with panic. He clutched at his sizable jowls, dropping his gun in the process. Collins quickly knocked it away with his foot, then twisted Victor's wrist counter-clockwise, straightening his arm out as he turned it against the shoulder joint. He pressed his other hand onto the elbow sharply, forcing him down. Victor's face collided with the hood of the rental, smashing his nose. A thin spray of blood painted the side panel.

Offering no opportunity for respite, Collins unleashed a heavy kick, burying his shin deep into Victor's ribs, feeling them break. Victor wheezed and coughed as he sank to the ground. He struggled to rest on all fours, spitting more blood out in front of him.

Collins placed his foot on top of the fingers on Victor's swollen hand, applying enough pressure to restrict his movement. "Listen to me, ya fat sack of crap. I said I'd get ya the money, and I will. I believe in paying my debts, however big they are. But if ya threaten me again, I'll break your damn neck. Understand?" He paused to examine Victor's head. "Assuming I can find it, that is..."

He quickly stomped his foot down, breaking every finger on Victor's hand. Victor screamed as he rested back on his considerable haunches, cradling his newly-broken bones.

Collins glanced at his car, seeing the fresh bloodstain dripping down the paintwork just above the wheel arch. He frowned, momentarily angry, before turning and thrusting his knee hard into Victor's face, connecting with the already-broken nose and making the bad wound worse.

"And *that's* for bleeding on my car, ya bastard! I'll lose my deposit if I can't get that clean..."

Behind him, he heard a screeching of tires. He looked

over his shoulder to see another car appear, sliding to a stop. Three men got out, each one dressed as Victor was, and produced a gun from inside their respective suit jackets.

Collins sighed, holding his hands out to the sides as he muttered, "Ah, bollocks..."

One of the men stepped forward, standing close to him. He was the same height, with the same tanned complexion as Victor, but was well built, muscular—a far cry from his colleague.

"Ray, don't make this any harder on yourself," he said. "Get in the car."

Collins kept his eyes locked on the man in front of him, stalling while he figured a way out of the situation. He could see the other two men in his peripheral. They were too far away to rush. They would shoot him before he managed two steps. The guy in front of him could be taken out easily enough, but he had to think of the consequences. There were a lot of people around, most of them watching in morbid fascination.

He couldn't see a viable way out of it, and he knew he had no choice but to go with them.

"Lead the way, asshole," he said with a resigned shrug.

With all three guns aimed at him, they escorted him over to their vehicle, pausing beside it for a moment while one of them frisked him. They took his cell phone from his pocket, tossed it to the ground, and stamped on it before forcing him into the back seat. One of them got in beside him, keeping his gun trained on Collins the whole time. The one who spoke rode shotgun.

As the driver started the engine, he turned to the man next to him. "What about Victor?"

The man looked out at their rotund colleague, lying motionless next to Collins's rental, and shrugged. "Screw him. He couldn't get the job done. Let him walk back. He could use the exercise anyway."

Behind them, Collins smiled to himself as they pulled out of the hotel parking lot, soon immersing themselves in the sea of traffic along the boardwalk. He had no idea where they were taking him, but he knew he was surrounded, unarmed, and cut off from any of his friends.

6

Collins did his best to keep track of where they were going, noting any road signs or landmarks they passed, but it soon proved futile. Five minutes into their journey, a thick, black bag was placed over his head. He had asked if it was necessary, but the reply had simply been a stiff punch to his gut, so he figured it was.

Instead, he focused on the time. He reckoned they had traveled for almost a half-hour before the car slowed to a stop. He was ushered out of the vehicle and frog-marched to his right. The temperature had risen significantly during the journey, and the heat inside the bag was taking his breath away. It also emphasized the musty smell surrounding him, which was almost unbearable.

"Guys, it stinks in here," said Collins, coughing. "You don't need to keep me covered up, all right? I know how stuff like this works. I won't say anything to anyone."

He felt a sharp blow to the back of his head, followed by a deep voice that said, "Shut up, asshole."

They weren't walking long before the man at his side, holding his arm, said, "Watch the steps."

Collins slowed, carefully moving his foot forward until he felt the first one with his toes. He heard his escort move behind him as he climbed. He was still outdoors and could feel the warmth from what little breeze there was on his arms. He counted seventeen steps before the ground leveled out again. Another hand gripped him, shoving him to his right. His footsteps were suddenly muted, and the natural sounds of the outdoors faded away.

A few seconds later, he felt a hand on either shoulder spin him around and force him down into a chair. It was soft and comfortable, and the cool leather was a welcome reprieve for his exposed skin. The bag was snatched from his head, and he blinked hard against the sudden influx of artificial light, so his eyes would take less time to adjust.

He glanced around, quickly realizing he was on a plane —a private jet, to be precise. His seat resembled an armchair, and he counted only eight of them inside, including his. He looked up and down the aisle beside him, seeing an armed sentry at either end.

No way out.

The chair directly opposite him was occupied. Collins started from the bottom, first noting the plush, cream carpet lining the floor. Then he saw the shiny, black heels; the long, smooth, caramel legs, crossed right over left at the knee; the short, black leather skirt that left little to the imagination; the manicured hands, clasped patiently in the lap, adorned with expensive-looking jewelry; a loose-fitting white top, barely clinging to the surgically-enhanced breasts; and finally, the most beautiful face he had ever seen—deep red lips curled into a smile that was half-amusement, half-arrogance and hypnotic, seductive brown eyes bordered by cropped, jet-black hair. It was a face he had seen before, but despite the stunning exterior, he wasn't happy to be seeing it again.

He slumped slightly in his seat, looking away as he sighed. "Hey, Patty."

Patricia Velasquez un-crossed her legs and shuffled slightly in her seat before re-crossing them the opposite way. "Hello, Ray."

Her voice was low and alluring, with a gentle, nasal Hispanic tone. She was known as Patty only to those she had given her consent. To everyone else, she was Miss Velasquez, and she was one of the most feared and respected businesswomen on the East Coast. Her numerous holding companies served as reputable fronts for her real dealings, which included gunrunning, money laundering, and the importing and exporting of drugs.

"You owe me fifty thousand dollars, Ray," she said.

He leaned forward, resting his arms on his legs. "I know I do, Patty. I'm trying to scrape it together, but the interest is killing me. If ya can just give me a little more time..."

She sat forward, matching his body language.

"Ray, me and you, we... we go way back, right?" She reached over and placed her hand on his arm. "We used to be very close, and I understand why we're not anymore. But I need *you* to understand something. This is business. I've given you as much time as I can, but I have my own interests to protect, not to mention my reputation."

Collins sat back, taking a deep breath. He didn't feel afraid, but he was aware the situation was getting away from him, and it wasn't about to start getting better.

"I can get ya what I have by tomorrow," he said.

"Which is... *how much*, exactly?" she replied.

He shrugged. "About nineteen, maybe nineteen-five."

Velasquez sat up straight in her chair, her expression

hardening as she narrowed her eyes. "And the other thirty-plus grand? You've had almost two months, and you haven't even got half of what you owe me."

Collins was quick to pick up on the sharpness and impatience in her tone. "Hey, cut me some slack, Patty. Two months ago, I only owed seventeen. Ya bought out my debt from that other prick and then cranked up the interest. I could afford to pay *him* back."

"And yet, you didn't. I was doing you a favor, Ray. Don't turn this around on me. You got yourself into this mess."

"How is *this* a favor? I went from owing seventeen thousand dollars to nearly fifty in eight weeks, by doing absolutely nothing!"

She relaxed back in her seat. "It was a favor because Ramirez didn't have the patience—or the soft spot for you—that I do. When I heard about the problems he was having with you, you were three days late, two grand short, and for that, he was about to put a price on your head."

Collins squirmed a little in his seat, pausing to glance out of the window beside him. "Okay, I didn't know that, and I'm grateful, truly. But I just can't get my hands on that kinda money. Not without risking it all, which would be pretty stupid."

Velasquez nodded. "I agree."

"So...?"

She shrugged. "So, that's your problem, Ray, not mine. Our history notwithstanding, you're leaving me with very little choice here. Now I've been more than fair so far, and I think I'm keeping very calm under the circumstances. So, this is what's going to happen. I'm going to step outside and spend fifteen minutes smoking a cigarette and enjoying the lovely weather. You can sit here, in peace, and think how you can get me fifty thousand dollars in the next twelve hours. If, when I return, you're still out of ideas, I'm going to put a gun to your head and pull the trigger. Do I make myself clear?"

Collins let out a painful sigh. "Aye... *crystal.*"

"Good."

She leaned forward and kissed him on the cheek before getting elegantly to her feet and leaving the jet, escorted by two of her armed bodyguards. Collins watched her go, then rested his eyes on the remaining three men, who were all watching him from a respectable distance.

Velasquez wasn't stupid. He knew that. He figured those men wouldn't be tempted to get close enough to him that he could disarm one of them and fight his way out. He also had little doubt they would shoot him if he tried, regardless of how much money he owed.

He sank back in his seat, sliding down a little to rest an elbow on the arm and his chin in his hand. He gazed out of the small window beside him, staring blankly across the runway. The heat shimmered on the blacktop, and there was no wind to counter it. He shook his head and sighed as he glanced at his watch.

He needed to think of something.

In what felt like no time at all, Collins heard the muted steps of heels on the expensive carpet behind him as Patty Velasquez returned from her cigarette break, lowering herself with a natural seduction into the seat opposite him. He leaned forward, resting his elbows on his knees, and held her gaze. Her dark eyes stared back with practiced allure.

"Well?" she asked.

He sighed. "Patty, listen... I—"

She held up a hand and smiled apologetically. "D'you know what? For now, I think it might be best if you refer to me as Miss Velasquez. Just so there's no confusion over the current status of our relationship."

Collins flicked up a questioning eyebrow. "Are ya being serious?"

She said nothing. She simply smiled.

He rolled his eyes. "Fine. Whatever. *Miss Velasquez*... I think we both know I can't get ya fifty thousand dollars by tomorrow."

She nodded along as he spoke, as if she understood what he was saying but didn't understand why he would be saying it.

"So... what are you saying to me, Ray?"

"Well, first off, I think it would be best if ya referred to me as Mr. Collins... y'know, so there's no confusion about the current status of our relationship."

In a flash, Velasquez lunged from her seat and wrapped a manicured hand around his mouth, squeezing his cheeks together, so he resembled a goldfish. He grimaced as her long nails dug into the skin of his face. She rested her other hand on the arm of his chair and leaned over, putting her face close to his.

"You may be attractive, Ray, but you were never the brightest, so I will keep this simple for you. If you ever get cute with me again on *my* plane, in front of *my* men, I will rip your goddamn balls off and wear them as earrings. Do you understand me?"

Her voice was low and as soft as her accent would allow. He nodded as much as he could in her surprisingly firm grip.

"Good." She kissed his cheek and sat back down opposite him, taking a moment to compose herself. "Now... you were saying?"

He ran a hand along his jaw, opening and closing his mouth to relax his face. "I was saying... I obviously don't wanna disrespect ya, but I don't wanna die either. So, I have a proposition for ya."

Velasquez leaned on the arm of her chair and rested her chin lightly on the back of her hand. "I'm listening..."

He shifted in his seat, searching for comfort that the situation wouldn't allow. "I'll do a deal with ya. A straight swap. You wipe my slate clean in return for a favor from me."

Her eyes narrowed. "That sounds like a much better deal for you than me, honey. You might want to try again."

He smiled nervously. "Let me explain. See, I'm a... I'm a talented guy. Ya know that. I'm a skilled and experienced soldier with access to resources at GlobaTech ya can only dream of. I reckon I'm *exactly* the type of guy someone in your line of work wants owing them a favor."

Velasquez crossed her legs slowly, her tanned skin shimmering in the light from the window. She held his gaze for a long moment, her expression betraying nothing.

Collins shifted apprehensively in his seat, silently praying to whoever might be listening that he had done enough to see another sunset.

Finally, she sat back and grinned. "Now *that* is a deal we could both benefit from, Ray. Kudos for thinking on your feet. Now that I think about it, there is this one niggly little issue I've been dealing with for a while. I assumed it would cost me well over fifty thousand dollars to hire someone professional enough to resolve it for me, but with you... well, I think I've gone and bagged myself a bargain."

Collins sank into his seat and looked away. "Yeah... aren't ya lucky?"

She stood and held out her hand. "Come on. Let's celebrate our new business arrangement. Lunch is on me."

He took her hand and got to his feet, standing closely beside her. "Whatever you say, Miss Velasquez."

She gripped his face again, just like before, except this time, it was playful. "Oh, Ray, you're adorable." She kissed him on the lips. "Call me Patty."

She walked away toward the exit.

Collins watched her go, transfixed by her confidence and beauty, despite the situation. He ran a hand through his hair, took a deep breath, and followed her.

"Bollocks," he muttered as he stepped off the plane.

7

Jericho sat calmly in the corner of Hyatt's office. Hyatt was working feverishly on a spreadsheet, and the silence he required made Jericho uncomfortable. He fixed his gaze on a small stain on the carpet and focused on it, allowing his surroundings to fade from consciousness, retreating into his own world while simultaneously remaining alert and aware.

It wasn't an easy thing to do, but it was a technique he had picked up during his time with the CIA, from an old friend who had served as a sniper during a couple of missions together in Afghanistan. They had been shooting the breeze over a beer one night when the conversation turned to their military work. The sniper had mentioned being on a mission in Helmand Province that had required him to lie motionless on a mountainside for fifty-one hours. Jericho had commented that he couldn't comprehend the stress that would put on your mind. His friend had smiled and said that in those situations, he meditated to stay both relaxed and focused. Jericho hadn't understood it at first. His idea of meditation was a bunch of tree-huggers in some backwater forest retreat surrounded by marijuana and yoga mats. But his friend had been patient and explained the technique to him. It had stayed with him ever since and had proved useful more than once.

Julie was doing a lap of the floor. The office area formed a large circle, with a bank of elevators in the middle. They already had Hyatt's itinerary for the next few days, so they knew who to expect and when, but as an extra precaution, they took turns walking a circuit of the office floor, once every ninety minutes.

"Goddammit..." muttered Hyatt, pulling Jericho back to the reality of the here and now.

He looked over. "Is there a problem?"

"Yes, there's a goddamn problem! Ever since your so-called *experts* did... whatever the hell it was they did to my computer, it's been running slowly. I can't get anything done when this piece of crap takes ten minutes to sync with the company's servers."

"Well, I'm not an expert with computers," replied Jericho. "But I *am* an expert when it comes to counter-intelligence and surveillance. Nothing our Technical Support team did would slow down your system. I can promise you that."

Hyatt let out a heavy sigh. "It's just going too slow..."

There was a knock on the door. A second later, it opened, and Hyatt's secretary walked in. Jericho watched as she strode confidently toward the desk. She wore a different outfit than the day before, but he still thought she looked nice. However, remembering Julie's reservations from when they arrived yesterday, he found himself trying not to look, despite Julie not being there.

"Here are the documents you requested, Mr. Hyatt," she said, handing him a small pile of papers.

He took them without looking up from his screen. "Thank you."

She turned to leave, locking eyes with Jericho as she did. Her smile was more friendly than professional. Jericho responded in kind and watched her leave. A moment later, the door to the office opened again, and Julie walked in. She saw the resigned look on Hyatt's face and raised an eyebrow. "Everything okay in here?"

"Everything's fine," said Jericho. "Mr. Hyatt is frustrated by his computer's lack of processing speed."

"It was fine before your team messed with it," Hyatt mumbled generally.

Julie cleared her throat. "Mr. Hyatt, I'm not a computer expert, but I know surveillance and counter-intelligence. Nothing our team of technicians did would impact the performance of your system. I can guarantee you that."

He looked up slowly from the screen and stared at her. His blank, deadpan expression spoke volumes.

She turned to Jericho and shrugged. "What?"

Jericho smiled. "That's what I said. Almost word-for-word, which is pretty scary..."

She rolled her eyes and smiled back.

Hyatt stood and gathered some papers. "I have a meeting to get to. Tell the driver to bring the car around."

His tone was sharp and laced with frustration. Jericho looked over at Julie with a bemused smile. He could guess what her reaction to Hyatt would be.

Julie frowned and let out a taut breath. "Mr. Hyatt, I'm not sure which one of us you were just speaking to, but you would do well to remember that neither one of us is your damn secretary."

He looked up at her, scowling at her response. "Excuse me? *You* would do well to—"

"Save it," she said, holding up a hand to cut him off. "Don't take your pissy little mood out on me, okay? We're not your employees. I'm sorry your computer's not working, but the only reason we're here is to keep you safe. Not to summon your driver, get you a coffee, or kiss your ass. Am I clear?"

Hyatt was on the back-foot, shocked by her outburst with no idea how to respond.

"Well, yes. I mean, I—"

"Good. And if you talk to me like that again, the Mexicans will be the least of your worries. Now this meeting... it's at The Sinclair, correct?"

He nodded. "That's right. My client, Mr. Silva, insisted we meet in a neutral location to further discuss our business at the port."

"Okay then. Here's what's going to happen. When we arrive, you're going to remain in the car with my colleague while I assess the location for any threats or security issues. Only when I'm one hundred percent happy with it will you join me. Clear?"

He went to speak again but stopped, settling for a silent, compliant nod.

"Good," she said before looking at Jericho. "You set?"

Jericho got to his feet, straightened his suit, and joined her by the door. "As if I'm going to say 'no' after that?"

He stepped out of the office and to the side, waiting for Hyatt to follow. A moment later, he appeared, briefcase in hand, his shoulders slumped and a sad expression on his face. Jericho kept pace alongside him as they headed for the lifts, while Julie stayed two steps behind them, a wry smile on her lips.

8

———

The Sinclair was the in-house restaurant of a luxurious five-star hotel in downtown Montreal. It looked unassuming from the outside—a tall, plain building situated halfway along a cobbled backstreet behind an office block. Yet, inside told a different story. Wall-to-wall opulence attracted the highest standard of clientele, regularly including Ulysses Hyatt.

The limousine pulled to a stop in front of the entrance—two large glass doors with the name of the hotel emblazoned across them in gold lettering. A concierge stood to attention beside them.

Julie stepped out first and held the door almost closed as she scanned up and down the street. It took a full minute for her to convince herself there were no threats. She shuffled aside and opened the door, allowing Hyatt to finally join her. He nodded to her courteously, refraining from voicing any frustrations.

Jericho climbed out the other side and walked around, mimicking Julie's routine to satisfy his own professional paranoia before bringing up the rear as the three of them filed inside the hotel. They moved efficiently across the lobby toward the restaurant entrance on the right, opposite the front desk.

They were greeted by a head waiter, who smiled at Hyatt as they approached.

"Monsieur Hyatt, welcome back," he said, extending his hand. "We have prepared your usual table."

Hyatt shook his hand courteously and nodded a greeting. "Thank you, Pierre. Has Mr. Silva arrived yet?"

"Not yet, sir. Would you prefer to wait in the bar area for him?"

"No, thank you. We'll take our seats..." He trailed off, glancing apprehensively at Julie. "If that's okay?"

She's trained him well, thought Jericho, trying to suppress a smile.

Julie gave Hyatt an appreciative nod. "Just give me a sec."

She moved past Pierre and stepped into the restaurant. It was a large, square room, flooded with natural light from the windows that ran the full height of the right-hand wall, offering a view of the street outside. She frowned, thinking how easy it would be for someone to drive past and take Hyatt out.

The doors leading in from the lobby were central on the near wall. As the room opened out in front of her, a long, vertical counter divided the space a third of the way along. It looked to be for serving buffet food. The rest of the room made ample use of the space, with minimal seating in favor of more privacy for diners.

In the far-left corner, she saw doors leading into the kitchen, which she noted would need checking.

She sighed. It wasn't where she would have chosen to

meet Hyatt's client had she been asked her opinion, but she could make it work. She stepped back out into the lobby.

"It's clear," she announced before looking at Hyatt. "I'll do a sweep of the kitchen area while Jericho sees you to your table—which..." She turned to the head waiter. "...I must insist is as far away from the windows as possible."

He flashed a questioning glance at Hyatt, who answered with a silent, almost imperceptible nod. Then he smiled at Julie. "But of course. Mr. Hyatt's usual table is our most private. If you would follow me, please."

He led the three of them inside, Hyatt sandwiched between Julie and Jericho, and over to a table positioned against the far wall. It was flanked by two large indoor plants, level with the kitchen entrance, and far enough away from other tables that any conversation was unlikely to be overheard.

As Julie disappeared into the kitchen, Jericho guided Hyatt to the seat facing the large windows. Should any potential threats approach the hotel, Hyatt would recognize them quicker than Jericho could assess them, so seeing his reaction could save valuable seconds.

Hyatt ordered a glass of iced water. When Pierre left, he took some papers from his briefcase and began reading. Jericho stepped away to a respectful distance and stood ready, his hands clasped in front of him, his eyes constantly scanning both the room and the street outside. After a couple of minutes, he placed a finger discreetly to his ear, activating his comms unit.

"How's it looking in there, Jules?" he asked quietly.

There was a momentary hiss of static before she answered. "Yeah, it's clear. No external entry points. Minimal staff. Heading to you now. Any sign of the client?"

"Nothing yet. I just—hang on... this might be him now."

Jericho watched as a well-dressed man in a fitted blue suit approached the head waiter's lectern in the lobby, followed by a single bodyguard. He saw the brief, muted conversation between them before the new arrival looked inside the restaurant, locking eyes with him before spotting Hyatt.

"Yeah, he's here now," whispered Jericho.

Julie appeared a moment later, walking past him and moving to the opposite side of Hyatt's table as Darius Silva approached, having left his own security guard in the lobby. He was a handsome man, oozing natural charisma. His subtle, styled hair and his well-groomed stubble simply added to his charm. He was also a known criminal and wasn't ashamed to admit it, should anyone ask. His fortune came from importing and exporting narcotics, and his influence stretched almost the full length of the east coast, branching out as far as Nova Scotia. He had a minor operation just south of the border, in Vermont, but crossing into the United States was risky, and the venture was still very much in its infancy.

He ignored both Julie and Jericho, simply smiling at Hyatt as if they weren't there.

"How are you, Ulysses?" he asked as he took a seat opposite him.

"I'm good, thank you. And you?"

Silva nodded. "I am very well. Business is good, but tension is mounting. Tell me, are we all set for tomorrow?"

"We are," confirmed Hyatt. "The cargo ship is due to dock around four p.m. It will depart again at nine-thirty."

"Excellent. I have arranged for my private jet to fly us there. We should arrive a little after five, which allows us plenty of time to finalize things."

"Of course." Hyatt looked past Silva momentarily, trying

to catch Julie's eye. He did and gestured her over with a subtle nod. "Miss Fisher, I would like to introduce you to my client, Darius Silva. Darius, this is Julie Fisher, head of my security detail from GlobaTech Industries."

Head of security, scoffed Jericho silently. *Since when?*

Silva grinned, his dark eyes sparking with life as he brazenly admired Julie from head to toe. He stood and extended his hand.

"It is a pleasure, Miss Fisher." He paused to kiss the back of her hand as she shook it. "I have never seen security look so... dazzling."

Oh, please... thought Jericho, resisting the urge to roll his eyes.

Julie smiled politely and took a step back as Silva took his seat once more.

"Good to meet you, sir," she replied professionally. She turned to Hyatt. "Is everything okay?"

He nodded. "Yes. I just wanted to make you aware that we'll be travelling to Halifax tomorrow afternoon aboard Mr. Silva's jet. In case you needed to make any preparations."

Julie raised a slight eyebrow and glanced over at Jericho. He responded with a gentle shake of his head. She turned back to Hyatt. "I'm afraid that's out of the question."

"May I ask why?" said Silva smoothly as he shifted in his seat and leaned on the table, looking up at her.

She shrugged. "You can ask..."

His expression hardened. The charm left his eyes, reducing their spark to an impatient glimmer. He went to speak again, but Hyatt held out a hand, silently asking him not to react.

"Miss Fisher," Hyatt began. "We can work with you to address any concerns, but I'm afraid we must—"

"Uh-uh. *We* mustn't do anything," she replied. "I understand you have work to do, but you will have to make alternative travel arrangements. I'm not putting you on a private plane that we have no control over. There are too many risks involved. Too many X-factors."

Silva's expression had softened again. His politician's smile had returned, and the charisma was oozing from him as if controlled by a faucet.

"Miss Fisher, if I may? I am happy to allow GlobaTech Industries to provide a pilot, if that helps?" He got to his feet again, holding her gaze as he smiled. "I appreciate my business and my reputation may be of no concern to you, but you need to understand that both are of great concern to me... and to Mr. Hyatt. We both need to be at the Port of Halifax tomorrow afternoon. It is too long a journey by any other means."

Jericho moved over to the table, stopping beside Julie. Silva's attention was drawn to him. He stared first at the fifty-inch chest. His smile faded as he lifted his head to look him in the eye.

Jericho narrowed his gaze as he locked eyes with Silva.

"Our concern," he began, "is Mr. Hyatt. That's it. We don't much care about anything, or any*one* else. Though it's worth mentioning that not too long ago, I was being shot at by members of a Mexican cartel as I tried to rescue our client's daughter, who was kidnapped by people who *did* care a great deal about *your* business."

Silva took a small step back. "And you have my sincerest apologies, as does my friend, Ulysses. That was unfortunate."

"Just a little, yeah."

Jericho instinctively flexed his shoulders, the sudden tension triggering his own defense mechanisms.

Silva, whether it was to his credit or his detriment, didn't flinch.

"I have the utmost respect for what you people are doing over at GlobaTech. I do. You're helping to shape a brave new world for everyone. But do not forget your place. You're a security guard. Nothing more. Do you think your size impresses me? I am a very powerful man, Mr..."

"Jericho."

"...Mr. Jericho, and I am not easily intimidated. It is in everybody's interest that we work together here. I need Ulysses to make sure my business transaction goes off without a hitch. In turn, you want to keep him safe. I have extended an olive branch to you, which I suggest you take. Otherwise, my friend will find himself in the market for a new security detail."

Julie stepped in front of Jericho the second Silva stopped talking. With last night's bar fight still fresh in her mind, she had no wish to jeopardize their work because Jericho had broken someone in half.

She cleared her throat and smiled. "Mr. Silva, speaking as the only woman here, I can say with complete confidence that there is far too much testosterone flying around right now. I think we should all just take a breath, don't you?" She glanced over her shoulder at Jericho, gesturing with her head for him to step away, which he did, albeit reluctantly. She turned back to Silva. "Now, I suggest you sit down, order your food, and have your meeting with our client."

After a moment, Silva took his seat, composing himself as he took his napkin and laid it across his lap.

"Will you join us?" he asked Julie.

She smiled politely. "You have things to discuss. And I have a job to do. I need to be ready should anyone storm in this hotel and try to kill you both."

Before he could reply, she moved around the table and stood a respectful distance away, as Jericho was opposite. They exchanged a small smile as Silva and Hyatt ordered their food.

This is going to be a long couple of days, thought Julie.

9

Three thousand miles away, Moses Buchanan stood resting against his desk, watching a live feed being streamed from a helmet cam on the monitor opposite. The helmet belonged to a unit commander who was leading a team of GlobaTech military personnel on a U.N. peacekeeping mission in Cambodia.

Two days ago, members of the Royal Thai Armed Forces were conducting routine checks along the border just north of Krong Poi Pet. A truck driver refused to present his paperwork and, when pressed, opened fire, killing two Thai soldiers. The truck was pursued back across the border into Cambodia, where it was picked up after a few miles. The driver was taken into custody but was uncooperative with the Thai authorities.

The goods he was transporting were traced back to a factory in Phnom Penh, owned by a shell corporation. Official documentation on the company was yet to be located. At first glance, the cargo seemed harmless, but further investigation determined they were key components of a prototype explosive device.

The United States government was reluctant to get involved, due to their fragile relationship with Cambodia, but the concern over a new weapon and a potential attack could not be ignored. And so, the call was made to GlobaTech, who were able to send their own forces to investigate in an official, neutral capacity on behalf of the United Nations. Due to the sensitive nature of the mission, Buchanan was personally overseeing it.

He looked on as the unit swept through a warehouse connected to the factory. It appeared deserted and empty, save for a few remaining boxes of raw materials. The lighting was poor, but the hi-res display allowed him to see with impressive clarity. Patches of damp on the floor were barely visible, having been all but absorbed by the dust.

As the unit turned a corner, something caught his eye on the screen. He activated the comms on the earpiece he was wearing.

"Back up a minute," he said, moving toward the screen for a closer look. "There. On your left."

The unit commander's feed moved as he turned, scanning for what Buchanan had seen. After a moment, the screen rested on a fragment of a wooden crate with markings on it.

"That's it," he confirmed. "Can you get any closer?"

"Copy that, sir," replied the commander, who crouched and picked it up, holding it to the camera.

"What's that?" queried Buchanan. "Some kind of logo?"

"Not sure, sir. It looks like a small triangle. It's clearly a section of a larger design. Honestly, it could be anything."

Buchanan sighed. "Yeah, okay. Forget it. Finish your sweep, log anything you find, and get your asses back home. Beers are on me for a job well done, Commander."

"Copy that, sir."

The line went dead. He removed his earpiece and placed it on his desk beside a remote, which he then used to turn off the monitor. He sat in his chair and reached for some papers. A second later, the light on his intercom started flashing, and a buzzing sound broke the fresh silence in his office.

"What is it, Kim?" he asked, pressing the button.

"I have Jericho Stone for you on line one," she replied from outside.

"Put him through." There was a click as the call connected. "Jericho, everything all right?"

"So far, I guess, yeah."

Buchanan grinned. "Wanna try sounding a little more convincing?"

Jericho chuckled. "Sorry, boss. Jules is having a tough time getting Hyatt's client to do what she wants. And I'm having a tough time not ripping his damn head off. There's a little tension here, but the client is secure, which is what matters."

"Why do we care what his client is doing?"

"That's a long story. I'll skip to the end. I know you're busy. We need a private jet to take us from Montreal to the Port of Halifax tomorrow afternoon, approximately thirteen-hundred hours. That a problem?"

Buchanan rested back on the hydraulic suspension of his chair, bouncing lightly as he ran a finger over the bridge of his nose. After a moment's silence, he said, "How important is this?"

Jericho sighed. "In terms of protecting Hyatt while he finishes the job that got his daughter kidnapped, it's a deal-breaker, boss. His client *kindly* offered to use his own jet, but there are obvious risks with that."

He rolled his eyes. "Yeah, all right. It's not like it's *my* money paying for it or anything. I'll get Kim to arrange it. She'll text you the details."

"Thanks."

"Everything else okay out there?"

"Yeah, nothing to report. We've studied a layout of the port, so we have a basic idea of what we're walking into now. Hopefully, it'll stay this quiet. Any word from Ray?"

"No, but you know him. He's probably locked away in some hotel room with a couple of young ladies, not giving two shakes of a sheep's joy department about either of us."

They both shared a laugh.

"I'll check in again tomorrow morning," said Jericho. "We should be done here within forty-eight hours."

"Good work. I appreciate you taking this job, Jericho. I know it was short notice, and I know the client's a pain in the ass, but he's a big-money contract for our private security sector, which is why I wanted to use my own personal unit for it."

"No explanation needed, sir. I'm a soldier. I go where I'm told."

"I know, but still... Pass on my thanks to Fisher too, would you?"

"Sure thing, boss."

Buchanan ended the call and pressed the buzzer to speak to his secretary. "Kim, I'm going to send you the details for a jet that Jericho and Fisher need for tomorrow. Can you arrange that ASAP, please?"

"Of course, sir," she replied.

"Thanks. And no more calls today, okay? I've got a mountain of things I need to read and sign and try to care about."

"No problem, Mr. Buchanan. Will you be leaving early today?"

He checked his watch. He tried not to stay any later than six and never left any later than nine. It was a little after four.

"Nah, I'll stay here, maybe order take-out in a little while. You can finish for the day though."

"I finish when you do, Mr. Buchanan. You know that."

He smiled to himself. "Yeah. You're a good girl, Kim. I don't know what I'd do without you."

"Good enough for a pay rise, sir?"

He rolled his eyes. "Good enough to eat some Thai food that your boss buys you."

She giggled. "That'll have to do."

He put the receiver down and turned his attention back to his paperwork. For a moment, his mind wandered to Ray Collins and the company he imagined he was keeping.

"Lucky sonofabitch," he muttered to himself, smiling.

10

I should never have left Alyana, thought Collins as he stared across the table at Patty Velasquez.

They were sitting at a private table on the balcony of a restaurant overlooking Miami Beach, shaded from the afternoon sun by a large blue and yellow umbrella. Four men wearing dark suits formed a wide and impenetrable perimeter around them. Collins found himself feeling sorry for them, to an extent. Their suits were fitted and smart, their earpieces and wires were visible, their black sunglasses tight on their faces—professional security through and through. But it was in the low eighties, despite the shade, so he couldn't imagine how hot and uncomfortable they must feel.

Velasquez put a forkful of steak into her mouth, dabbing the corners of her lips elegantly with a napkin as she chewed. Collins didn't have an appetite. Instead, he sipped at a glass of scotch on the rocks, trying to relax.

He felt angry with himself for allowing the situation to spiral so dramatically out of his control. He knew he was better than that. He made one mistake, and he was paying the highest price for it.

He owed Patricia Velasquez.

"Are ya gonna tell me what ya want me to do?" he asked with a hint of frustration.

Still chewing, Velasquez held up a finger, wagging it side to side. She took her time swallowing her food before taking a long sip of her red wine, which left a faint lipstick mark around the rim of the glass.

"Patience is a virtue, Ray," she replied.

He felt a small smile creep across his face, triggered by a sudden fond memory of the two of them he couldn't ignore. "Since when have ya known me to be virtuous?"

She held his gaze for a long moment before returning the sentiment. "Fair point. That's one of the things that attracted me to you."

"There were more?"

She leaned forward, resting her elbow on the table and her chin on her hand. She stretched a long, tanned leg out in front of her and began moving her foot up the inside of his leg. Her smile widened. Her eyes softened.

"There were many, *many* more..."

Collins knew better than to think he could charm his way out of the situation, but he figured there was little harm in playing along. Perhaps appealing to her sense of nostalgia might buy him some grace.

He took a slow gulp of his drink as he felt her foot reach his knee. He rested both hands casually on the table, eager to demonstrate his restraint.

"Well, if ya ever fancy a little trip down memory lane, I could probably force myself."

She laughed playfully. "Only a little trip?"

"Aye. For now. We can always stay for longer if ya want?"

"Hmm, maybe. The only thing is..."

In a sudden and precise movement, she lunged across the table, grabbed her steak knife, and stabbed it into the wooden surface between two fingers on Collins's right hand. A millimeter either way, and it would have pinned him there.

"Jesus!" he yelled, flinching in his seat.

"...you are a lying, conceited piece of shit who owes me fifty thousand dollars! Not to mention three months of my life!"

He retracted his hand as she took her seat again, instinctively checking everything was still attached.

"For Christ's sake, Patty!" He looked around. The bodyguards seemingly hadn't noticed the sudden ruckus. "What d'ya mean, *three months of your life*?"

"I *loved* you, you arrogant sonofabitch!" she hissed. "And you left me in Paris without so much as a goodbye."

"In Paris?" He thought a moment, struggling to recall what she was referring to. When he remembered, he said, "C'mon, Patty, that was seven years ago."

"Not for me."

He held her gaze, staring into dark eyes that smoldered with a frantic hatred. But behind all that, he saw something else. He saw vulnerability. He saw sadness.

He saw a little girl with a broken heart.

He glanced away and sighed heavily. "Look, Patty, I—"

"Miss Velasquez," she said sternly, cutting him off.

He waved a hand, dismissing it. "Whatever. Ya know damn well why I left, so don't give me the puppy dog eyes and the sob story, all right?"

A single eyebrow twitched above her eye. That was the only thing close to a response from Velasquez. She held his gaze silently. Defiantly.

"And d'ya know what? I'm done being intimidated by ya," he continued. "I know ya too well. I owe ya money, I get that. I've said I'll do whatever it takes to clear the debt, and ya know I will, Patty. Ya have my word."

She scoffed and rolled her eyes.

He pointed a finger. "Hey, I ain't ever lied to ya, Patty. Think what ya want about me... say what ya want about me... that's the truth and ya know it. Could I have handled Paris a little better all them years ago? Sure. Probably. If I broke your heart, I'm sorry. But I ain't never lied to ya. Not once. All I have in this world are my word and my balls, and I don't break either of them for nobody."

She managed another fifteen seconds before her expression broke, and she started laughing. She threw her head back and slapped the table.

"Did you *really* just quote *Scarface* to me?" she said with a wide smile.

Collins shrugged with a sheepish grin. "Well, we *are* in Miami. Besides, ya know it's my favorite film. Pacino was dynamite!"

Velasquez leaned forward and extended her hand, placing it softly on his forearm. "You're right. I apologize."

He pulled his arm away and sat back in his chair, his eyes wide with surprise. "Say what now?"

She matched his body language and shrugged. "I said I'm sorry. You're right. I know exactly why we broke up, and I know why you left. We both agree that you handled it like an asshole, but I understand you felt you had no choice."

"*Felt* I had..." He shook his head with disbelief. "Patty, you were a criminal. Ya still are! Back then you were just an ambitious young thing trying to build the enterprise ya have today, and ya know what? I respected ya for it. I respected the hell out of ya for it. Ya know I haven't always been the boy scout that sits before ya now, but I've never been an idiot. I was working for the British government. When I discovered my mission was to investigate *you*, I had to leave, Patty. I *had* to. I couldn't bring myself to... I always..." He looked away and sighed. "Ah, forget it."

She finished her wine and cleared her throat. "I've been unprofessional. Seeing you again, it... it brought up some old feelings. Perhaps some issues I hadn't dealt with. But it's all in the past. We should focus on the present. And more importantly, whether or not *you* have a future."

Collins shifted uneasily in his seat. The moment of nostalgia, such as it was, had passed.

"Just so we're clear," he began, "I do this one thing for ya, and my slate's wiped clean?"

She smiled playfully. "Maybe..."

"No. There's no *maybe*, Patty. Ya know who I work for, right? Ya don't have long before someone notices I ain't come back from my vacation. You could be as big as Capone, and it wouldn't protect ya from GlobaTech's reach. Not now, and especially not if ya piss them off."

She held up a hand. "Relax, Ray. You'll have a heart attack. Of course, I know who you work for. I'm not stupid. This is a one-time deal... double or nothing."

He nodded. "Well, okay then. So, let's not beat around the bush. Ya want me to kill someone, don't ya?"

"Correct. Is that a problem?"

He shook his head. "If it's between me and some random criminal on your shit-list, I'll gladly choose *me* every time. Morals be damned. Who's the target?"

"He's a business rival. A very well protected business rival. I'll be honest with you, Ray. For a job of this magnitude and significance, I would normally hire a professional."

He rolled his eyes. "No, please, don't feel like ya have to butter me up or anything..."

She shrugged. "You're talented, Ray, but you're not a pro. Not at tasks such as this. In an ideal world, I'd hire the best. I'm getting a real bargain by essentially paying you fifty thousand for this. Someone like... I don't know... like Adrian Hell would have charged me four or five times that. Such a shame he retired..."

Collins couldn't resist a smile. "Whatever he's doing nowadays, Patty, I can promise ya one thing—that fella won't ever retire."

She narrowed her eyes with curiosity. "You say that like you know him?"

"I wouldn't say I know him. We worked together once, briefly."

She leaned forward, clasping her hands in front of her, beaming with excitement. "Really? Do tell!"

"No, I couldn't. It was..."

"Oh, Ray," she began, pouting with her full, red lips. "Did you make the mistake of thinking I was asking?"

He sighed again. "It was nothing. A couple of years ago, back when my boss was his best mate, I helped him cross the Belarusian border into Pripyat."

"What for?"

"As I recall, he was rescuing his girlfriend from a bunch of terrorists."

"Wow. So, you two fought side by side?"

"Not really. I got him across the border, gave him a shotgun, and left him to it."

"Oh."

He shrugged. "Like I said, we worked together briefly. Twelve hours or so, that was it. Nice bloke though. My kinda fella, y'know?"

"So, did he get his girlfriend back?"

Collins chuckled. "Aye, ya could say that. The bad guys were holed up beneath an abandoned hospital. Way I heard it, he acquired himself a tank and blew the whole place to pieces while playing 'Black Betty' through the PA system. Then he breached the underground facility, killed about twenty of the bastards, and walked back out the front door hand-in-hand with his lady—barely a scratch on either of them."

Velasquez laughed. "Jesus... I *really* wish I could hire *him* for this instead of you."

"Again, don't feel ya have to spare my feelings or nothin'..."

"Well, come on, Ray, seriously—how does anyone compare to that?"

She held his gaze, smiling mischievously. He smiled back as he realized she was simply trying to get a reaction from him.

"Yeah, yeah, all right," he said. "I ain't the jealous type, love. And I certainly ain't jealous of him."

She raised an eyebrow. "Really? Why not? He's so much... *better* than you."

"Well, that's a matter of perspective, darlin'. He's better than me at being a hitman, yeah. Obviously, he is—he's better than everyone at that. But I ain't trying to be a hitman, so that's an irrelevant comparison. I'm probably better at golf than he is, but I doubt he's ever tried to improve his backswing, so who the hell cares? I'm just sayin'... that guy has some issues."

"Ooh, gossip! Spill!"

He rolled his eyes. "Hardly. I just mean he has his demons. He's a fella capable of extreme focus and violence, yet he has this kinda... I dunno... Zen-like acceptance of his abilities. It's a little unnerving, truth be told. I respect the hell outta him, don't get me wrong, but if ya ask me, that bloke needs some serious therapy."

"Well, you learn something new every day..."

"Look, can we quit with the sleepover talk and get to the point, so I can be done with this?"

She nodded and sat back in her chair, as if someone flicked a switch and she was suddenly a ruthless criminal again.

"Before I can send you on your way, there's something I need from you."

Collins gulped what remained of his scotch, savoring the mild burn as it traveled down his esophagus. "Uh-uh. What did we just agree on? This is a one-time thing, Patty. I ain't jumpin' through any hoops for ya."

"You misunderstand me," she replied, holding up a hand and smiling apologetically. "I know the job is a one-time deal. If you're successful, your slate is wiped clean, we're square, and there's no need for us to ever cross paths again."

"Right..."

"But for me to agree to *give you* the job... to *give you* the chance to pay your debt... you need to do one small thing for me first."

"Fine," he muttered, sensing the futility in any further arguing. "Name it."

"I need you to apologize."

He frowned. "For what?"

"For leaving me in Paris."

"I thought we were past that?"

"Yeah... see, I thought we were, but then you told me that story about Adrian Hell, how he went to war for the one he loved. It reminded me of how I felt about you and how much you hurt me. And I want you to say sorry."

Collins shifted in his seat. "Well, not wishing to split hairs or anything, but I kinda did that already. Literally about two minutes ago."

"Yes, you did. But that was right before you quoted an Al Pacino movie, so I don't think you were being serious."

"Right now, I don't think *you're* being serious..."

Her expression hardened in an instant. "Be careful, Ray. I'm being *very* serious. In fact, as we speak, a very talented professional in my employment has a high-powered rifle aimed at you. Purely a precaution, you understand. But unless you make me believe your apology, your debt will be wiped for a completely different reason."

"That's bollocks," he said, shaking his head. "I know ya, Patty. Ya ain't that crazy."

She took out her cell phone, dialed a number, and muttered something inaudible when it was answered. A second later, a small red dot appeared on Collins' chest. She gestured to it, and he looked down.

His shoulders slumped forward as he realized he had mistakenly underestimated Patty Velasquez.

"Ah, shite..."

She smiled. "As I was saying... I'm going to need you to apologize."

Beads of sweat formed on his brow. He shifted again in his seat, contemplating making a break for it. He looked around. After a minute of indecision, he concluded he wouldn't get very far.

"Christ, Patty, this is crazy. Can I just—"

She whispered something else into the phone, and a heartbeat later, the empty glass in front of Collins exploded with a high-pitched ping.

"Jesus!" he yelled, flinching again.

Velasquez shrugged. "No, you can't *just*... anything. You

don't have the money you owe me, Ray. You already offered to do this job, and this task is a precursor to that agreement. Please don't make the mistake of interpreting the casual nature of this meeting as a sign you have any kind of choice in this."

Collins took a long moment to assess everything. The guards. The red dot on his chest. The sincerity in Velasquez's voice.

Finally, he let out a long breath, resigning himself to the fact she was right.

"Fine. Patty, I'm sorry. I am. I was an asshole, and I regret any hurt I caused ya. Okay?"

She shook her head slightly, as if not understanding.

"Who?"

He cursed to himself and gritted his teeth. "*Miss Velasquez*, I apologize."

She glanced away, playing absently with her hair as she stared out at the coast before them. Then she said, "No, I still don't believe you."

"Shite!" he hissed, squirming in his seat.

"D'you know what I think it is? I think it's the fact you're sitting opposite me, like an equal. Like we're on the same level. I just can't see past your arrogance." She pointed to the space next to their table. "Kneel and say it."

He exhaled a taut breath. "Are ya kidding me?"

"Do I look like I'm kidding you?"

He looked into her eyes. She didn't.

He slowly got to his feet, adjusting his T-shirt and looking around as he felt the embarrassment growing. He moved beside her and lowered himself to one knee, as if he were proposing. He checked to see if the red dot had stayed on him.

It had.

He tensed his jaw muscles, begrudging every second of what she was making him do.

"Miss Velasquez," he began. "I'm really sorry I broke ya heart all them years ago. It never would've worked between us, but there were a million different ways I could've handled it that were better than the way I did. Do ya forgive me?"

She held his gaze and took a deep breath. Then she got to her feet and raised a leg, resting the point of her stiletto heel on the soft flesh of his shoulder, close to his neck. Her skirt rode up, revealing even more of her tanned thighs, but Collins made a conscious effort not to let his gaze wander to what was inevitably on show to someone in his position. He locked his eyes on hers, grimacing as she applied more pressure with her heel.

"Don't ever forget what I just made you do," she said to him. "I have the power to make a man like you literally *beg* for his life. You would do well to remember that."

She lowered her leg and stepped away, giving him room to stand. As he did, he looked around again. The bodyguards hadn't acknowledged anything, but he still felt ashamed of himself. He composed himself, then stepped casually toward Velasquez, moving to the side as he placed a hand gently on her waist.

He leaned in close, as if kissing her cheek. With his mouth next to her ear, he whispered, "Just so ya know, *Patty*, when we're square and my debt is paid, I'm gonna make ya pay for that."

His tone was firm. It was respectful, but there wasn't any of the playfulness in his voice that he usually spoke with. He was deadly serious, and she knew him well enough to know he meant every word.

She moved her lips next to his ear, kissing his cheek. In a low, sultry voice, she replied, "I can't wait."

She moved away and clicked her fingers. One of the bodyguards came over and took a cell phone from his pocket, which he handed to her before walking away.

She held it out toward Collins, who took it without a word.

"Keep this on you at all times. I'll send you details of the target and their location within the hour. How you do it is up to you, but I will have eyes on you the whole time, so don't try anything cute. You will have a small window of opportunity in which to carry this out, which will be explained in the message. Any questions?"

He looked at the phone before sliding it into his pocket. "Do I get a gun?"

"This task is as delicate as it is important. It absolutely cannot be traced back to me. I will not be risking exposure by supplying you with anything. You want a gun, find one."

He sighed. "Fine. Whatever."

She brushed past him and was immediately surrounded by the four bodyguards. As she walked away, she glanced over her shoulder and winked back at him.

"Happy hunting, my love." She nodded toward his crotch, and in her best Al Pacino accent, said, "Say hello to your little friend for me."

He smiled sarcastically but said nothing. He watched her leave and sat down at the table. He looked down to see the red dot had disappeared from his chest.

He let out a tired sigh as he took out the phone and rested it beside him on the table, next to a large shard of what used to be his glass.

"Shite."

11

Once Hyatt's meeting with Silva had concluded, Jericho and Julie had accompanied him back to his office, where he completed his day in virtual silence. Jericho had spoken with Buchanan during one of his patrols around the floor. Julie, meanwhile, had tried to coax some more information out of Hyatt about what to expect at the port, but hadn't managed to get anything useful.

Back at the hotel, Hyatt was safely installed in his room, and Jericho and Julie divided their time into hour-long shifts, alternating between guarding Hyatt and watching the entrance in the lobby.

Jericho cracked his neck to ease some built-up tension as he leaned against the doorframe of Hyatt's room, staring along the corridor ahead of him that led to the elevators. He hadn't seen anyone since his latest shift began.

He glanced over his shoulder toward the large window behind him, at the opposite end of the hallway. Outside, the final traces of natural light were fading, and the low cloud that had threatened rain throughout the day stubbornly held the moon's glow at bay.

He checked his watch.

Ten minutes left.

As he was thinking how great it would be to get in bed, there was a hiss of static, and Julie's voice sounded through his earpiece. "Hey, Johnny. You there?"

Jericho straightened, immediately alert, tensing every inch of his body.

He, Julie, and Collins had a system in place where they used fake names on comms if there was danger and they were compromised. He was Johnny.

Something was wrong.

"I'm here, Kate," he replied. "How's everything in the lobby?"

"All quiet. There was a slight rush of evening check-ins about twenty minutes ago but nothing that worried me. Most exciting thing that happened was when an old lady asked me for directions because she thought I worked here."

"If it stays that uneventful, I'll be a happy man."

There was a pause.

"I was thinking," Julie began. "We should get away for a few days, just the two of us."

"Yeah?"

"Yeah. I know it hasn't been long since we got back from our last trip, but we had such a *blast* there, didn't we? Sitting by that *fire*, *shooting* the breeze... Plus, I know Ray enjoyed it. That cute young *girl* took a real shine to him, didn't she? We should go back there. Or, if we can't, at least get a room together somewhere... party a little, maybe bring a piece of that place to us. I guess I'm just feeling the *pressure* right now, and it would be nice to get away, y'know? Do you know what I mean, Johnny? Does that make sense? Or do you think I'm crazy?"

He took a deep breath, processing everything she had said.

"You're not crazy, Kate. I understand you completely. And I feel the same. I would love to visit there again. Relive some of the excitement. Why not come up to the room now? We can start the party early."

She sighed with relief. "I thought you would never ask, big guy."

The line clicked off again.

His vision blurred as he stared blankly at the wall in front of him, his jaw tensing, his brow furrowed, his fist clenched as he tried to make sense of what was happening.

He knew exactly what she meant.

Her voice had an unnatural edge to it, and the way she spoke was deliberately strange. It was rigid and awkward, and she emphasized words that didn't need it. And, most importantly, she talked about the two of them being together—something she hadn't ever—and likely never would—talk about.

He took a short moment to decipher their conversation.

Sitting by the fire... Shooting the breeze... Collins with a young girl...

She was talking about Mexico. No doubt.

Bringing a piece of it to us... Feeling the pressure...

People from Mexico were at the hotel. There had to be more than four, because any less and Julie would have kicked their asses. Whoever they were, they had a gun on her, and they could hear the conversation.

He refocused and subconsciously tapped his hand against the weapon he had holstered beneath his jacket. They would be coming for him any moment. He didn't have much time.

In the lobby, the hustle of late check-ins had died down. Two people sat behind the front desk, one speaking into the phone while the other worked away at the keyboard. A young couple walked leisurely across the far side of the lobby, heading for the bar and pulling small suitcases behind them, laughing together.

Ten minutes earlier, five Hispanic men had walked through the doors. They had huddled together, talking discreetly between themselves while conspicuously looking around at the positioning of the security cameras and personnel. Then they had split up, all taking seats close to the front desk but sitting separately, spread out across the middle of the lobby.

Julie was standing close to the staircase that led to the second floor, leaning against a wall beside a large, circular indoor plant, idly flipping through the pages of an old magazine. She was alert while expertly blended in with her surroundings.

She clocked the group of men almost immediately. Her suspicions weren't raised at first. She merely noticed them arrive. But their body language and behavior soon put them on her radar. She had watched them take their seats, noting the strategic positioning. She went to activate her comms, to let Jericho know of a potential threat, but at that moment, she felt the unmistakable touch of a gun barrel press against her lower back. The coldness of the steel penetrated her jacket.

The unseen sixth man had ushered her toward the others, pushing her into the seat beside one of the men while keeping his gun discreetly hidden by his jacket. He had then explained to her that they knew who she was, and they knew her partner was guarding Hyatt. He had told her to make contact on comms and, without alerting him, persuade him to go to his room and leave Hyatt unprotected. If she didn't, they would shoot her in the head where she sat.

As far as they were concerned, she had done as they asked.

"There," she announced. "He's going to meet me in my room. Hyatt should be alone now."

"Very good," said the man with the gun, nodding his approval with the faintest of sneers on his face. "You should be an actress, y'know?"

Julie shrugged. "I'd rather be anything than a bodyguard right now."

"You are funny. You're a funny lady," he laughed. He leaned forward and brushed a loose hair from her face, which Julie did her best not to flinch at. "It's a shame I'll have to kill you."

She frowned. "Huh? Why? You just said you'd shoot me if I *didn't* do what you asked. You can't then say you'll shoot me anyway—that doesn't make any sense."

He fell silent. His smiled faded. His gaze hardened.

"You talk too much. Nervous?"

She shrugged again. "Not really. I just like to understand the people I'm eventually going to punch in the face. And right now, I understand you guys are amateur hour."

He straightened, gesturing with the gun in his pocket. "You should probably stop talking now. Time to go."

She folded her arms across her chest and crossed her legs, raising a challenging eyebrow. "Not until you tell me what you want with Hyatt."

"What difference does it make to you?"

"Hey, if I'm going to die protecting his ass, I at least want it to be for a good reason."

He sighed. "Because I'm being paid to take him to see my boss and his business partner, and my orders are to dispose of anyone who gets in the way."

Julie nodded. "So, is your boss the head of the cartel I shot the hell out of a few days ago, near the Mexican border?"

The wave of rage that crashed across his face was sudden. His eyes burned with split-second fury. He lashed out, slicing the back of his hand across her face. The crack of the contact resonated around the mostly-deserted lobby. The people behind the desk looked over, concerned. The man glared at them until they looked away, then turned his attention back to Julie, who was wincing against the sting of the slap.

"You *really* do talk too much. I'm thinking once I've killed your partner and retrieved Hyatt, I might spare you. I could use some... entertainment for the trip home."

Julie rolled her eyes. "Listen, you piece of shit. If it's the last thing I ever do, I would make damn sure I ripped off anything you put near me, are we clear?"

She held his gaze, the venom in her eyes matching the anger in his. After a long, tense few seconds, he looked away, addressing one of the other men in Spanish. A moment later, she was hauled to her feet and marched to the stairs.

"Which floor?" asked the gunman.

"Sixth," she replied.

He pointed to the stairs. "Move."

She watched as two of the men stepped in front of her. Two others moved behind. The gunman joined them, leaving one by her side.

Smart, she thought. *The gun isn't within immediate reach, and the stairs will make it hard to gain any tactical advantage before they can take me out. Very smart.*

Surrounded, she began climbing, hoping Jericho understood her message and was ready for war.

"I don't understand," said Hyatt. "You're supposed to keep me safe!"

Jericho sighed. "I am, Mr. Hyatt."

"How is *this* safe?"

After speaking to Julie, Jericho had entered Hyatt's room and explained the situation. He tried to stay as vague as he could, so he wouldn't cause too much panic, but Hyatt was stubborn—and a little stupid—so he was forced to tell him, in great detail, how a group of Mexican cartel foot soldiers had compromised Julie and were heading up to the room, presumably to kill the pair of them. The color had drained from Hyatt's face. He struggled to find any words but had managed to ask what Jericho intended to do about it.

His answer was simple: take them out.

But to do that, he had explained, he needed to make sure he didn't need to worry about Hyatt, should any bullets start flying, which is why he had insisted on him lying down in the bathtub.

"If you keep as flat and as quiet as you can," replied Jericho calmly, "you should be protected from any bullets in there."

Hyatt's eyes popped wide. "What do you mean, *should?*"

"Well... there are never any guarantees in a gunfight, but a thick, ceramic bathtub will offer more cover than a mattress." He took a breath, seeing from the look of horror on Hyatt's face that he wasn't doing a great job of reassuring him. He crouched beside the tub, resting on the ledge. "Look, a gunfight is all about odds. It's a numbers game. It's also played out mostly on instinct. I estimate there are five guys..."

"Why?"

Jericho shrugged. "Any less than five, Julie would've taken them out in the lobby."

Hyatt's eyes narrowed. "Jesus... really?"

Jericho smiled. "You've met her, right? Would *you* mess with her?"

"Hell no," he replied, chuckling humorlessly.

"Exactly. Now look at the location. That's a pretty narrow corridor outside. For five guys, there isn't much room to maneuver, which means they'll be forced to stack up in a line and file in through the door. They will keep at least one guy on Julie. Maybe two. Let's assume one, because that's the worst case—both for us *and* for the poor sonofabitch who's left with her. So, that's four guys who will storm this room. We have to assume they want you dead, which means they *definitely* want me dead. They will want to be fast and noisy, to create a sense of chaos and reduce the chances of me being able to react effectively. But these guys won't be professionals. They will think they are, but compared to me and Julie, they're the equivalent of kids in a playground, chasing each other and yelling *Bang, Bang*. I would say there's an eighty percent chance they will run into the room and empty their guns into the bed."

"Why the bed?"

Jericho shrugged casually. "Human nature. If you're in danger, where's the safest place you can think of to go? You go home. You get in your bed. You pull the cover over your head. It's something that's instilled in you as a child —your bed's the safest place in the world, right? It sounds crazy, but your brain is hardwired to stick with what it knows in a time of crisis. People who panic run to the safest place they can think of, which, believe it or not, is their bed."

"Wow... okay."

"Now, once the firing stops, they'll see you're not in there. Your room is a good size, but it's an open space, which means, realistically, there's only one more place you could be."

"In here?"

"Exactly. So, in the interest of time and with their limited training, they'll take aim at the wall and the door of the bathroom and open fire, aiming for your chest and head."

"I see..."

'But the mistake they will make... the mistake *most people* would make... is that they'll assume you're standing. So, if you stay low, statistically, you're much safer than if you didn't. They will finish shooting, kick the door open, and see there's no body on the floor. They will want to look behind the curtain. If they do, they will find you lying in the tub, and that's game over."

Hyatt sighed. "P-please tell me there's a but..."

Jericho nodded. "*But*... all that is assuming the entire situation has a chance to play out. It won't."

"So, you'll..."

"They'll all be dead or unconscious before they fire a single bullet."

"You sound confident. I thought you said there aren't any guarantees in a gunfight?"

"There aren't. But they won't get the chance to start firing, so technically, this won't *be* a gunfight. And I'm confident because I'm very, very good at what I do."

Hyatt lay flat in the tub, crossing his arms over his chest

as if he were in a casket. He let out a long breath. His expression relaxed.

"Thank you," he said.

Jericho got to his feet. "No problem. Now I'm going to pull the curtain around you. All you have to do is stay quiet... no matter what happens, no matter what you hear, okay?"

He nodded. "I... I'll try."

"That's all I ask."

Jericho pulled the curtain across and stepped out into the main room. As he turned to close the bathroom door, he heard Hyatt whimpering. The sound was amplified by the acoustics of the tub. He closed his eyes for a moment, then walked back inside.

"Mr. Hyatt, I... ah... I can hear you crying."

He heard a hard sniff behind the curtain. "I'm n-not crying!"

Jericho yanked the curtain open and stared down. Hyatt's eyes were bloodshot, and tears stained his cheeks. "Uh-huh..."

"Well, I'm sorry!" yelled Hyatt. "I'm not some insane, tough guy, super-soldier like you. I'm scared out of my mind, like any normal human being would be!"

"I understand that, Mr. Hyatt, and I'm sympathetic to your situation. But *you* need to understand that if you make a sound while even one of these assholes is still awake, you're going to die."

"Is that supposed to make me feel better?!"

"No, it's supposed to give you some perspective." Jericho took a short breath. "Okay, I know something else that might help. Do you want to try it?"

Hyatt nodded frantically. "Yes. Anything!"

"Okay..."

Jericho leaned over and delivered a short, precise jab to the side of Hyatt's jaw. It was barely at half-power, but it was enough to knock him out.

"There we go," he said to himself. "Nice and quiet."

He closed the curtain again and headed out of the bathroom, shutting the door behind him. He crouched around the slight corner by the bed and drew his own weapon. He wouldn't be seen by anyone until they were halfway into the room, and by that time, they would be within reach and the battle would be almost over.

He chambered a round and held the gun low and steady, his finger resting outside the trigger guard. He wouldn't fire unless it was necessary. He wouldn't kill unless it was necessary. But he *would* do whatever needed to ensure both Hyatt and Julie were safe.

He took a few deep breaths, allowing his mind to drift into its more basic, primal state.

"Come on, you bastards..."

Julie had reached the sixth floor, still flanked by the cartel soldiers. They had climbed the stairs in silence. She knew she had no move on the way up, so it was pointless trying anything.

They shuffled along until they reached the junction by the elevators. The wall ahead was dominated by a painting that looked like an ear of corn resting in a field. The corridor stretched away in both directions.

"Which room?" asked the gunman behind her.

"Eleven," she replied, pointing to her left. "This way."

The group started walking, giving her no option but to follow. Their footsteps were loud, despite the thick carpet.

Room eleven was roughly halfway along on the left. As they approached, Julie scanned the doors to the other rooms, wondering if Jericho was behind any of them. There was no sign of him in the hall.

They stopped outside the room, and the group of five moved into position, forming a shallow semi-circle in front of the door. The man with the gun stepped in front of Julie, a little ahead of her on her left. He took his weapon from his pocket. Julie noted the familiar shape and size.

A Glock, she thought. *Nice piece.*

She nodded to it. "I couldn't help but notice you don't have a suppressor on that thing. You know if you fire that, this entire building will be surrounded by SPVM in minutes. You won't make it out with Hyatt."

"Do you think I give a shit about the *policia* in this country? Bunch of pussies."

She shrugged. "Hey, whatever... it's your funeral. I mean, they're probably on their way right now. You weren't exactly discreet in the lobby."

He whipped his body clockwise, driving his fist into her temple. Her legs buckled as the impact forced the consciousness out of her, and she slumped to the floor. He then stepped into the semi-circle, shoving one of the men toward the door and taking his place.

"Open it," he said. "Let's get this over with."

The rest of the men reached into their jackets and retrieved identical Glocks. The sound of rounds being chambered filled the hallway. The man closest to the door took aim at the handle and brought his other hand up to his face as a symbolic shield.

Then he squeezed the trigger.

12

Jericho heard the loud ping of the gunshot and the sound of the lock popping inside the frame. He fought to keep his finger outside the trigger guard. To remain patient. He looked around the room—a final check of his surroundings; a final run-through of his plan.

The door flew open, hitting the side wall with a bang. He chanced a split-second peek around the corner. A flash that his subconscious mind was trained to scrutinize with inhuman efficiency. From his vantage point, he saw two men dead ahead, and the arm of a third to the right. Behind them, on the floor, he saw an outstretched leg and a shoe he recognized as Julie's.

"Sonofabitch..." he whispered to himself.

He heard the steps as the first of them entered the room. They were heavy and deliberate, with no clear effort of discretion. He listened closely, learning the speed and the rhythm of the first man through the door. The first casualty.

He held his breath, willing his heart rate to slow. To embrace the calm before the storm. The simmering of peace before an eruption of war.

The man's foot and leg appeared in his line of sight, level with the corner.

Jericho straightened, jumping up to meet the guy as he stepped into the room and slamming the thick part of his forearm, close to the point of his elbow, hard into the side of his head. The man never saw it coming. He barely registered the movement before it was too late.

The impact was dull and unforgiving. It sent a wave like an electric shock shooting up Jericho's arm and into his shoulder, such was the power behind the blow.

The man was knocked out almost instantly, but his body still flew into the near wall and bounced off the desk facing the bed before sprawling onto the floor.

One down.

He looked out into the hallway as two more men filed in through the open door. The first had his gun raised.

Jericho dove back around the corner as the first bullets whizzed past, chipping the plaster and splintering the thin walls inches above his head. He held his own gun out and fired blind, ensuring he aimed high to avoid catching Julie, whom he assumed was still on the floor outside.

He shot three rounds and heard the first guy hit the floor. A moment later, he slid into view, carried forward by his own momentum. His torso was stained crimson, his eyes wide with shock and fear. His gun had flown from his hand, but he stubbornly reached for Jericho, crawling slowly toward him along the floor as blood leaked all around him, like something from a zombie movie.

Jericho hesitated for a moment before putting another round in the man's head to finish the job. He didn't want to kill anyone unnecessarily, but the guy was mortally wounded and clearly suffering. The final bullet was a mercy.

As he scrambled to his feet, the second man ran into the

room, spear-tackling him onto the bed. The momentum and the bounce of the mattress carried them both over and onto the floor beneath the window. Jericho landed on his back, with the man on top of him, his *Negotiator* flying from his grip.

Jericho held onto the guy's left wrist with one hand, preventing him from wrapping their hand around his throat, while wrestling with the gun with the other, trying to disarm him. In the struggle, two rounds were fired before Jericho had the position and leverage to bury his knee into the back of his attacker. The impact sent him off-balance, and Jericho used the opportunity to roll him to the side while simultaneously shifting his own hips in the other direction. With the cartel soldier now on his back, Jericho pushed himself up into a crouch and delivered two hard punches to the guy's face. The first broke his nose. The second knocked him out.

Staying low behind the bed, Jericho quickly retrieved his gun and took aim at the door. Julie's leg was still visible, but there was no sign of anyone else. He figured they would be waiting on either side of the doorway for a chance to shoot.

In his peripheral vision, he noticed two bullet holes in the bathroom wall—the result of the stray rounds fired during his brief tussle moments earlier. They were in a near-perfect horizontal line, roughly two inches above the level of the mattress. The thin wall had done nothing to stop them. They had punched right through and into the bathroom. By his reckoning, at the same height as the bathtub.

"Ah, shit!" he grimaced.

He made his way around the bed, keeping low as he drew level with the bathroom door. He saw the feet of someone standing to the right of the room just outside.

"Screw this..."

He aimed at the wall inside the room, roughly waist height, and fired four rounds in quick succession. The first two laid the groundwork, violently chipping away at the plaster. The third and fourth forced their way through. A moment later, a body hit the floor in the hallway.

Another man emerged from the left, stepping into the room with his gun aimed high in an unsteady hand. Jericho anticipated it and stood to meet him, grabbing the outstretched wrist and pushing it down and left, allowing him to jam the butt of his gun hard into the guy's nose. The cartilage gave way beneath the impact with little resistance.

He always tried to aim for the nose. It's easy to break, restricts breathing, and makes the eyes water. If your opponent can't breathe or see, they are much easier to beat.

Jericho spun the guy around and gripped his neck, holding him still. Then he placed the barrel of the *Negotiator* to the back of his head and edged forward, ensuring he could check both directions before he committed to exposing himself in the openness of the hallway.

He peered around the doorframe to the right. There was a guy standing a few feet away, his gun trained on Hyatt's room. Jericho shifted his human shield to the left, protecting himself from the side he hadn't yet checked. As he did, he raised his own weapon and fired two more shots with rapid, lethal precision. The first bullet hit the man just above the knee. The second punched through the center of his chest, leaving a contained, dark red splatter on the wall behind him.

He immediately spun left, resting his gun on the right shoulder of his hostage as he hunched behind him.

He had miscalculated. There were six men, not five. The last one stood facing him, aiming a Glock from behind his own human shield. From behind Julie.

"Enough," said the man. "Give me Hyatt, or I kill the woman."

"Give me the woman, or I'll kill your guy," replied Jericho.

The man smiled. "Go ahead. I don't care about him."

Jericho believed him. He locked eyes with Julie. She was struggling to focus, having been dragged upright and conscious not a minute earlier. She was coming to her senses but not quickly enough.

A door opened to his right. A middle-aged man wearing a suit tentatively peered outside. Everybody turned to him.

"Sir, for your own safety, you should really stay in your room," said Jericho, firmly. "I'm with GlobaTech and I'm handling the situation, but feel free to call the police."

The man disappeared hurriedly back inside his room and slammed the door closed. Jericho re-focused on the gunman.

"You're running out of time," he said. "Who sent you?"

He shrugged. "What does it matter to you? You're worse than her. Give me Hyatt, or I'll shoot you both."

Jericho shook his head. "I can't do that. Give me the woman, and I'll let you live. That's my only offer."

The man laughed. "You need to work on your bargaining. Tell me, were you in Mexico a few days ago?" He nodded at Julie. "With her? Are you the ones responsible for killing so many of my brothers?"

Jericho shrugged. "I don't know. Who are you, and who do you work for? Tell me that, and I'll tell you if I killed any of your friends."

The man's eyes narrowed. "I work for Bernardo Cortez. Our cartel family controls the single largest territory in all of Mexico. And you... you killed a lot of my friends. Senor

Cortez will be very pleased if I bring him your head as well as Hyatt."

"Whatever. What does the cartel want with Hyatt?"

"He has information regarding a shipment we want."

"Right, so, your beef is really with Darius Silva? What if I deliver him to you instead? Will you let my friend go and leave without Hyatt?"

"Our beef is with whoever we're paid to have a beef with. Today, it's Hyatt. Darius Silva is nothing to us. But his shipment is important to Senor Cortez's business associate. I have orders to bring Hyatt back alive, so I'm bringing him back alive. End of story."

"Good to know. Thanks."

Julie stamped down on the man's foot, ducked, and drove her elbow into his gut. She broke free of his grip and sent him stumbling backward. The moment she was clear, Jericho put a single round in the man's head. He dropped like a felled tree, landing hard on the floor. A narrow spray of blood dripped down the wall behind him.

Jericho then smashed the butt of his gun into the back of his human shield's head, sending him tumbling to the floor. He then moved over to Julie, who was crouched a few feet away, just beside the door to Hyatt's room.

"You okay?"

She nodded. "Yeah, I'm good. Nothing a couple of painkillers won't fix. You?"

"I'm fine."

"Hyatt?"

"Good question..."

He stepped urgently back into Hyatt's room and opened the bathroom door. Two steps put him next to the tub. He yanked the curtain open and stared down at Hyatt. His eyes were still closed, but he could see the rise and fall of his chest. He checked the holes in the wall and followed the path the bullets would have taken.

There were two large punctures in the side of the tub. He leaned over and looked at the inside. Two cracks, like spiderwebs, were lined up level with Hyatt's body, but the bullets hadn't penetrated the ceramic.

Jericho closed his eyes and breathed a sigh of relief before heading back out into the hall.

"He's fine," he announced. "He's still out cold, but he's alive and unharmed."

Julie was sitting on the floor against the opposite wall. She frowned. "Why is he out cold?"

Jericho holstered his weapon and sheepishly scratched at the back of his head. "He wouldn't stop crying, and I needed him to be quiet, so..."

"So... you hit him?"

"Only a little bit."

She sighed and shook her head. "I don't even care. What do we do now?"

Jericho looked around at the sea of scattered bodies. "Well, I should probably call Buchanan and explain this to him. He'll be able to buy us some grace with local PD. I'll stash Hyatt in my room tonight. We should move him first thing in the morning. And you need some rest too. If the cartel has managed to track Hyatt, we have to assume they'll try again once word gets back that these assholes failed. I need you at your best."

She struggled to her feet and took a couple of uncertain steps. "No arguments from me."

Jericho chuckled. "First time for everything..."

She glared at him. "Hey, I can still kick *your* ass, big guy. Watch it."

He smiled as she walked away toward the elevators.

Behind him, he heard a groan. He turned to see one of the men he hadn't killed stirring on the floor. He moved over to him and pulled him to his feet, pinning him to the wall.

"You and I need to have a little chat," he said, smiling.

13

Moses Buchanan hunched over his desk, his palms spread across the surface. He stared blankly at the calloused knuckles. His vision shifted in and out of focus as his mind raced between his current crisis and flashes of his life before a desk, back when those knuckles hadn't yet earned their hardened skin.

Kim Mitchell was standing opposite, a respectful few steps away. She clasped her hands professionally in front of her and shifted her weight from one leg to the other as she waited patiently for her boss to say something.

Five minutes earlier, she had entered his office without knocking, distracted by the urgency of her message. He had a video call waiting for him. She had stayed with him as he took it, knowing he would need her once he was finished.

The call was from GlobaTech's liaison with the Royal Thai Armed Force. He was sitting behind a makeshift desk in the hangar of an airfield. The connection was unstable, which distorted the image, but Buchanan saw commotion behind him. The sound intermittently dropped in and out, but enough of the message came through.

The unit Buchanan had securing the warehouse in Cambodia had been attacked and killed by unknown forces. He had played the last feed received from the unit commander on a screen-in-screen feed. It showed them coming under attack. It wasn't clear from the commander's viewpoint where the attack came from. Within two minutes, the feed had dropped and fallen to the side as the commander was shot and killed. A moment after that, the sole of a boot had stomped on the camera, ending the video.

Buchanan had told his liaison to take point on the investigation, to lead a unit of Thai forces into the region and call every fifteen minutes with an update.

The call ended, and he had stood in silence ever since.

Kim waited to hear what he needed from her, but she knew he was taking this hard. She had been the personal secretary to Josh Winters previously, and she had adored him for the fact that he never let his position deter him from getting involved in the work GlobaTech was doing. Sometimes, he was too involved. He could have easily distanced himself from the day-to-day stuff, locked himself in board meetings, and collected a seven-figure salary. But he hadn't. He had personally commanded an elite unit that risked their lives on his word to make the world a better place. When Moses Buchanan had stepped into that role, he had very much continued Josh's legacy, and she adored *him* for that, too.

It just meant that, in situations like this, he couldn't help but hold himself accountable.

Finally, he looked up at her. His eyes were heavy with the burden of guilt. "I'm gonna need you to—"

His landline started to ring, interrupting him. He reached for it, but Kim stopped him.

"Let me handle it," she said, leaving no room for argument. "I'll take a message."

She answered but didn't get chance to speak. The voice on the other end began relaying their reason for calling. She nodded along, waiting for an opportunity to talk.

"Okay... I understand... just let me..." She sighed. "Jericho, will you shut up for a minute?"

She raised her voice, startling Buchanan. The line fell silent.

"Thank you. Let me pass you over." She held the receiver out toward Buchanan. "It's Jericho."

"Yeah, I figured," he replied, reaching for the phone.

"He sounds stressed."

"Great..." He placed the phone to his ear and turned to stare out of his window. "Jericho, now isn't the best time. I need good news, or I need a break."

On the other end, Jericho cursed himself for not considering what else might be happening in his boss's world, despite his own situation.

"What's wrong, sir?"

Buchanan sighed. "Nothing. Bad day at the office. What do you need?"

"Well, we've got a situation here. I... Are you sure you have the time for this? I can always—"

"What do you need, Jericho?" he said, his tone hardening.

"Right." He cleared his throat. "We just got hit."

Buchanan turned, staring at Kim as if doing so would help share the surprise. "What? Are you hurt? Is Fisher okay? What about Hyatt?"

Jericho smiled to himself. That's what he admired most about his superior. When shit hit the fan, he always ensured his employees were okay before he asked about the job.

"We're all fine. Jules took a bad knock, but she's okay. There were six of them. They got the drop on her in the hotel lobby. They came up to the room looking to take me out and leave with Hyatt."

"Goddammit. Any idea who they were?"

"Yes. They were Mexican. Members of the Cortez cartel. The same group who took Hyatt's daughter. The same group we shot the hell out of the other day."

"How in the blue hell did they find out where you were?"

"Good question. One I intend asking when this asshole wakes up."

"You've got one of them?"

"There were two left alive after the skirmish, sir. I've brought one of them to my room. I had to hit him again, so I'm just waiting for him to come around."

"Are you not relocating?"

"No, I think it's better to stay here until morning. I don't want to risk a mobile firefight, should we leave. I've no idea if these assholes who hit us had back-up. At least here, we're now surrounded by police."

"Makes sense," nodded Buchanan. "What about Hyatt?"

"Hyatt's with me too. Jules is resting up. I hate to ask, but could you..."

"...smooth things over with Montreal PD? Yeah, no problem."

"Thank you. I'll liaise with them as soon as I'm done here. There are a lot of bodies and bullet holes that need explaining and scared guests that need reassuring. It's gonna be a long night. Sir, I know this is a shit-storm you don't need right now. I take full responsibility, and you can reprimand me when all this is over."

Buchanan smiled to himself. "At ease, soldier boy. Just

finish the job and get your asses home safe. I'll make sure the cops work with you, not against you."

"Thanks, boss."

Buchanan terminated the call and handed the receiver back to Kim.

"What do you need?" she asked.

He took a moment to think, glancing at the blank monitor as he processed everything that had just happened. Finally, he said, "I need you to push everything on my schedule back a couple of days. I don't want any more calls unless it's Jericho or our guy on the ground in Cambodia. I also need to speak with the director of the Montreal Police, so I can explain away Jericho's latest attempt at foreign diplomacy."

Kim let slip a small smile. "Right away, sir."

She turned to leave, but Buchanan called after her. "Oh, one more thing, Kim."

She glanced back as she reached the door. "Yes?"

"Get a hold of Collins for me, would you? I've a feeling Jericho and Fisher are gonna need all the help they can get."

She nodded and left, leaving Buchanan alone in his office. He sat heavily in his chair, resting his head in his hand as he leaned on the arm of it.

The airport remained busy, despite the late hour. Collins stood in a short line for the ticket booth and checked his watch. Velasquez had told him she would message him the details of his target, including the location, once he was at the airport, but as yet, he had received nothing.

He shuffled forward.

"You're cutting it fine, Patty," he muttered to himself.

No sooner had he spoken, his cell phone began to ring. He didn't realize it was his at first because technically, it wasn't. His had been destroyed when Victor and his boys had picked him up earlier that day. This was the phone that Velasquez had given him.

He took it out and answered.

"Yeah?"

"You took your time," said Velasquez impatiently. "You're not busy, are you?"

"I'm in the line at the airport," he replied, refusing to rise to any bait. "Where am I going?"

"I've just sent you the details. When you land, a mutual friend will meet you. He'll help you secure the right tools for the job."

Collins frowned. "But I thought ya said…"

"I'm feeling generous. Don't make me change my mind by trying to be charming or funny."

He rolled his eyes. "Yes, ma'am."

"Our friend will also keep you company while you do the job. To make sure you don't get lonely."

"Christ, Patty. I don't need a goddamn babysitter."

"Well, that's not really your decision now, is it?"

"Fine. Do ya want me to call when it's done?"

"That would be lovely, Ray. Would you mind?"

The sarcasm wasn't difficult to miss.

"Not at all, Patricia. Bye for now." He hung up. "Bitch…"

He shuffled forward again, putting himself one person away from being served. He checked his messages and quickly read the name of the target, where he would find him, and where he needed to fly to.

After a moment, he approached the desk. The woman behind it smiled at him admiringly. She had light brown hair tied up in a ponytail and wide, happy blue eyes.

"Good evening, sir," she began professionally. "Where are you flying to today?"

Collins was quick to pick up on the attraction. It was something he counted himself blessed to be used to. He leaned on the counter and smiled.

"Hey, darlin', I need the next flight ya have to Halifax, Nova Scotia, if ya would?"

She swooned at his accent as she tapped away on her keyboard. She checked his passport and his shoulder bag, then printed his ticket and boarding pass.

"That's gate fifteen," she said. "Enjoy your flight."

He smiled politely. Courteous without being humorous. "Thanks, darlin'. It'll be the trip of a lifetime, I'm sure."

He winked and walked away, not needing to look back to know she was watching him go.

As he navigated the steady crowds, he took out his phone and looked over the details Velasquez had sent him once again. Then, satisfied they were committed to memory, he deleted them from the phone.

"Well, Mr. Darius Silva..." he muttered, "I hate to be the one to tell ya this, but you're about to have a very bad day."

14

***

The pale morning light pushed through the vertical blinds hanging at Julie's window. She sat cross-legged on her bed, dressed for the day, despite the early hour, in a fresh trouser suit. She had slept well after the events of the night before and felt rested enough to deal with whatever the new day had to throw at her.

At the foot of her bed, Jericho paced back and forth across the room, like a caged animal impatiently waiting to be unleashed. Unlike his colleague, he hadn't slept much, although he hadn't really tried to. He had spent most of the night interrogating the cartel soldier he took to his room. He hadn't known much, but Jericho had persuaded him to spill everything he *did* know anyway. Then he'd turned him over to the local authorities, who had quickly secured the hotel during the night, following the shootout. Buchanan had called to say he had spoken with the SPVM, and they would be extending them their full cooperation.

Julie had already been down to the lobby that morning to speak with the police still on site, to give them GlobaTech's official statement.

Hyatt lay sprawled on the sofa beneath the window in Julie's room, doing his best to stay awake but struggling against his own body's primal urge to shut down.

"So, what do we know?" asked Julie.

"We know the cartel was hired by someone with a vendetta against Darius Silva," said Jericho. "Someone who wants this shipment of his. And we don't know how, but whoever it is also seems to know Hyatt is a factor—and a potential weak link in all this, which is why he's now been targeted twice."

Julie nodded. "What do you think we should expect at the port?"

Jericho shrugged. "After last night, who the hell knows? My gut says whoever's hiring the Mexicans knows about the port, but they don't know when exactly the shipment is arriving, or when and how it's leaving. If they did, they wouldn't be pursuing Hyatt so aggressively. If it were me, I'd have people in place all day today, morning till night."

"That makes sense. That's been the main issue all along here—that we don't know what we're walking into once we arrive at the port."

"Well... hope for the best, prepare for the worst, right?"

She arched a brow. "Since when did you subscribe to fortune cookie wisdom?"

He smiled back. "Since this job turned into a grade one shit-show where people keep shooting at us."

"Well, this particular SNAFU aside, we need a plan going in." She nodded toward Hyatt, who had drifted off to sleep again. "He's not going to make things any easier. And Silva is a wildcard. We have no control over him or his actions. I suspect, should bullets start flying, he'll care more about his precious shipment and his reputation than anyone in this room. If something happens and he retaliates, we'll be dragged into a firefight whether we like it or not."

"I agree," said Jericho tersely. "I'm beginning to lose my patience with Silva and his goddamn shipment. He's dragging Hyatt and us into his mess, yet we're the ones working our asses off to clean it up. It's bullshit."

"I know, but tolerating that asshole is a necessary evil if we want to make sure that little girl sees her daddy again."

"Yeah, you're right..." He stopped pacing. "We should get to the port as early as possible. Like, right now. Minimize the chance of anyone getting the drop on us."

"Sounds like a plan, big guy." She jumped to her feet and walked around the bed, stopping in front of Hyatt. He was sitting with his arms folded across his chest, low on the sofa, with his head lolled back against the cushions. He was breathing slowly. She watched him for a moment and then gently kicked his leg. "Rise and shine, sleeping beauty."

He jumped in his seat, startled. His eyes snapped wide open.

"Huh? What? Don't hurt me!"

She chuckled as he calmed down, slowly realizing his surroundings. "Not a real big moment for you there, huh?"

He seemed unfazed by any potential embarrassment. "I'm sorry, I..."

"Relax, Mr. Hyatt. We need to get ready to move, okay?"

He struggled to his feet, stifling a yawn. "I thought we were flying out later today? Why so early?"

"We're compromised here," said Jericho. "There's no point staying any longer than we need to. I'll take you to your room, so you can get your things. My colleague will make sure the plane is ready ASAP. We need you to get in touch with your client and tell him the change of plans."

"Oh, I'm not sure that's a good idea. Mr. Silva prefers to stick to his schedule. He won't appreciate having it changed on such short notice."

"Well, luckily for us," said Julie. "I don't give a—"

"What my colleague means," interjected Jericho, "is that your client needs to understand he's not as in control of this situation as he might like to think. He needs to trust us and, for once, just do what he's told."

Hyatt thought for a moment and then nodded. "I'll make the call."

"I appreciate that. Just tell him to get there ASAP. Nothing else."

As they headed for the door, Jericho stared at Julie, silently questioning her. She shrugged a silent *what?* and began gathering her own things, preparing to leave.

Jericho smiled to himself as he followed Hyatt out into the hall.

"Kim? Where the hell is Collins?" Buchanan shouted through the closed door of his office to his secretary outside. He sat slumped in his chair, staring at the surface of his desk, idly drumming his hands on it to a random tune.

He had just finished up a call with Jericho, who was about to step onto the jet with Fisher, Hyatt, and Hyatt's client, heading for the port in Halifax. He agreed with Jericho's assessment of the situation, instructing him to check in the moment they landed and when they reached the port itself.

He had told Jericho he was trying to reach Collins, to

send them some support, but it had been almost twenty-four hours, and every attempt had been unsuccessful. His cell phone was turned off, so they couldn't even track him via GPS. Like it or not, Collins was off the grid—much to Buchanan's displeasure. He had ordered his secretary to keep trying, but his patience was now wearing thin.

On top of that, he was expecting another call in the next five minutes from his liaison in Cambodia, with an update on the investigation surrounding the death of an entire GlobaTech unit.

Buchanan had admired Josh Winters a great deal, but it wasn't until he had stepped into his shoes that he truly appreciated how good the man was at his job.

The office door opened, and Kim appeared, leaning on the handle as she stuck her head inside the room. Her brow was creased with pressure.

"You have an intercom, you know?" she said tersely. "There's no need to yell."

Buchanan looked at her, moving only his eyes, so he was staring through his eyebrows. His hard expression said more than any words could.

Kim glanced away, giving herself a moment to regain some professional courtesy. "Maybe we'll... ah... look at how that works later."

"Still no luck reaching Collins?" he asked her, happy to ignore what he knew was never intended to be disrespectful.

She shook her head. "I'm afraid not. His phone is still turned off."

"Shit. Okay, keep trying, would you?"

She nodded. "Of course. But Mr. Buchanan, if I may..."

An intermittent beeping filled the room, interrupting her. The large monitor opposite flashed into life, and the words INCOMING CALL appeared on the screen.

Buchanan reached for the remote. Kim turned to leave.

"Could you stay for this please?" he called to her.

"Ah, sure. But isn't this confidential? Like, *above my paygrade* confidential, I mean?"

He smiled. "Well, first of all, I set your paygrade, so let me worry about that. Second of all, you're the secretary to the director, so there's very little of what I do you can't see. But third of all..." He paused, taking a slow, calming breath. "I've got a lot going on. A lot of balls in the air. This is important and I don't want to miss anything. I would feel better if you took some notes, to make sure I catch everything I'm about to be told."

She smiled back sympathetically. "Of course."

"All this with Jericho is bad enough, but this..." He aimed the remote at the screen and pressed a button to connect the call. "I've got a bad feeling about this one."

The screen flickered into life, and the face of the Globa-Tech liaison appeared with intense clarity.

"What have you got for me?" asked Buchanan.

The man shook his head. "Not much more than I had the last time we spoke, sir. But we do have something of interest."

"Tell me."

"The warehouse had a second security feed, retro-fitted and connected to an external server."

Buchanan frowned. "By who?"

The man shrugged. "Unknown, but we're assuming by the personnel working in the warehouse."

"Not by their employers?"

"We don't think so, no. The primary feed was linked to the main server house a few miles away, owned by the same dummy corporation that owned the warehouse. The paper trail is non-existent, which speaks volumes about the kind of people we could be dealing with here."

"We still don't know who runs this dummy corporation?" asked Buchanan. "Or who they're a subsidiary of?"

The liaison shook his head again. "I'm afraid not. Not yet anyway. I have some of the best people here working on it."

"Good. So, you were saying?"

"It's safe to assume whoever these people are, they're into something big. The tech we intercepted in the truck that led us here was high-end. Military grade. Not easy to get a hold of. But we think whoever was overseeing this particular operation installed a second feed, either for their own protection or at the request of another party. We don't know why, but we're not complaining."

"You've got the feed?"

He nodded. "We traced the feed to its source—the back of a local sweatshop maybe twenty miles away. Most of the equipment is still intact, but we could only retrieve three minutes of footage."

Buchanan thought for a moment, glancing at Kim for silent inspiration. Then he looked back at the screen and said, "It was a motion-sensor camera. Programmed to start recording if someone tripped a sensor or something."

"We think so, sir, yes. But, more specifically, a sensor above one particular door in the warehouse. The feed we found was linked to a tripwire above a fire exit in the northeast corner of the warehouse that was obscured by some crates—stacked up, we think, to cover it. It leads to a dirt track that disappears into some local jungle on the outskirts of the town. We figure it was there as a fast, anonymous way out, if needed. But the camera started recording when the door was opened."

"So, that's how the people who killed our guys got inside?"

"That's right. They were good but not good enough to detect the second feed, so we have footage of them entering and exiting the warehouse, before and after the attack on our people."

Buchanan moved around his desk and sat on the edge, taking a second to compose himself for what came next. "Show me."

The face of the liaison shrunk to a small window in the top left corner of the screen, overlaying the video that now dominated the feed. It was black and white and a little grainy, a far cry from the crystal HD display a moment ago but still good enough to see what was happening.

Playback began by the video flashing online, showing the fire exit mentioned a few moments earlier. It opened slowly, and a small team of men entered. Their movements were fast and deliberate, keeping in a semi-crouch as they moved as one cohesive unit. Four men. Two teams of two. All dressed in dark, unmarked outfits. Half-masks covered the lower half of their faces. Noses and mouths were hidden behind variations of a half-skull graphic.

As they moved out of view, the camera feed switched, tracking them as they moved like ghosts through the warehouse. Buchanan noticed the time stamp in the bottom right corner. What he was watching took place just ten minutes after his conversation with the unit commander yesterday.

The group split. Two moved left around a tall stack of empty metal shelving. The other two moved right, following the wall as it led away from their teammates.

"The sonsofbitches flanked them..." he muttered, transfixed on the screen. "They never saw them coming."

The feeds split as cameras activated to track each group. As Buchanan watched, he saw the second team of two stop as they neared another aisle of shelving. They each took a knee, waiting.

Then he saw a member of the GlobaTech unit step out, oblivious to the threat awaiting him. The muzzle flash was accentuated on the low-res video. As the light faded, he saw the GlobaTech soldier drop to the floor.

He heard firing from the other feed. He didn't need to look.

"All right, I've seen enough," he announced.

The feed vanished, replaced by the liaison's face as it filled the screen again.

"Any idea who those bastards are?" asked Buchanan.

"Unfortunately not," he replied. "The quality of the footage and the fact they're wearing masks make facial recognition impossible. We're trying to locate satellite imagery from the area around the time the assault took place, to see if we can track their movements on the way out, but so far, nothing."

Buchanan sighed with resignation. "Okay. Keep at it and keep me updated."

He clicked the screen off and tossed the remote across his desk before looking at Kim, silently asking for some direction.

"What do you think?" she asked him.

He moved behind his desk but remained standing. "Going off what we just saw, I would say they were mercenaries. Could be freelance. Could be on somebody's books. But looking at how they moved, it's as if they used to be military but have allowed their training to give way to bad habits. Albeit effective ones."

"What does that mean?"

He finally took his seat. "That means someone has hired a group of mercs to attack GlobaTech personnel. Those men weren't there for the warehouse. They were there for my team." He slammed his fist on the desk. "Dammit!"

Kim paused for a moment. "Should I call a meeting with the board of directors or the section heads?"

He shook his head. "No, not yet. For now, this stays in this room. Until I have something to tell everyone besides 'we just got attacked', there's no sense in causing panic. Some of the directors aren't *big picture* types."

"Understood," she said, nodding.

As she went to leave, Buchanan said, "You were going to say something before that call came through..."

She looked back. "Oh, no, it's nothing."

"Kim..."

She sighed. "Fine. Well, it was about the fact we can't get in touch with Ray. I was going to say, with everything Jericho and Julie are dealing with... and with all this in Cambodia... are we sure Ray is okay?"

Buchanan arched a brow. "You think he's in trouble?"

"I think we went from business as usual to def con three in less than a day. I think Ray is... a law unto himself sometimes... but he's one of the best we have. We both know that. He wouldn't go dark for this long without an explanation. Bad news comes in threes, so people say. I'm just worried his silence might be the third thing, I guess."

Buchanan smiled. He knew Kim had a soft spot for Collins, but he also knew she was the most professional person he employed. Not to mention incredibly intelligent and wasted in the role of secretary. He had learned very quickly not to ignore her intuition or concerns.

"I don't subscribe to superstition," he replied. "But I'm a

big believer in your instincts. Get on to our team of analysts, see if we can pick up his last known location. Just in case."

She nodded and smiled back. "On it, boss."

She left him alone, and yet again, Buchanan found himself staring out of the window behind his desk, out across the vast expanse of GlobaTech's main compound. He watched the small city bustle about its business, keeping the world in check.

"Whatever you're doing, Ray, I hope you're all right. We need all the help we can get right now."

Collins landed at Halifax Stanfield International Airport as the sun was rising on a new day. He hadn't managed to get much sleep on the flight, his mind occupied by the task that lay ahead of him. No matter how many different ways he approached it, he saw no obvious way out that didn't result in him looking over his shoulder for the rest of his life. He knew Patricia Velasquez well enough to know that he didn't want her hunting him.

Having only a carry-on bag with essential items for the trip, he was able to forego baggage claim after clearing passport control and head straight for the exit. The drastic change in temperature had hit him like a freight train. Gone was the high-eighties of Miami, replaced by the aggressive low-fifties of Nova Scotia.

Distracted with trying to mentally adjust to the new climate, he didn't see the man approaching him from his right. As he stood on the sidewalk outside the main entrance of the airport, overlooking the wide semi-circle reserved for taxis picking up and dropping passengers, he felt the familiar sensation of a gun barrel push into his side for the second time in as many days.

"Ah, bollocks," he muttered as he turned to address the new arrival.

The man was wearing a three-quarter length leather jacket over a high-neck charcoal gray sweater. He had a couple of days' growth on his face and throat and wore sunglasses, which Collins noted were certainly not required, so must be for added discretion.

"Let me guess," he said. "You must be the babysitter Patty sent me."

The man had smiled with little humor. "Miss Velasquez wants to ensure you carry out the job as expected, that's all."

"Uh-huh..."

"My ride's this way. It's an hour to the port. Let's go."

Not wanting to draw attention to them, Collins followed willingly. The man gestured him behind the wheel before sliding into the passenger seat.

They travelled in virtual silence. The only exchanges between them were when Collins received directions. The journey took closer to an hour and a half as they had hit some morning traffic along the way.

A five-story parking garage stood on a slight rise, over-looking the Port of Halifax from roughly five hundred yards away. Collins navigated them to the top floor, which was largely deserted. He nosed the car into a spot facing the port, close to the barrier at the edge. His babysitter then retrieved two traffic cones from the trunk, which he made Collins place at the bottom of the entrance ramp, so no other vehicles could come up, ensuring they had the privacy they required.

He then passed him a long, black bag, which contained a GlobaTech-issue sniper rifle. Collins was familiar with the weapon. He smiled at the man as he unzipped the bag and began assembling the long gun.

"This is meant to be some kind of joke, right?"

The man shrugged. "A little irony never hurt anyone, I guess. But at least you have no excuses when it comes to taking your shot."

"Aye..."

Once the rifle was ready, he found a comfortable spot that offered the widest possible view of the port and settled in for the long wait. He could see the entrance gates, where the main highway branched off and inside the yard. He could see warehouses and stacks of storage containers. He could see the foreman's office. He could see two docking lanes.

He let out a heavy sigh and waited.

Almost three hours passed.

Collins glanced to his left, where the man was sitting on the ground with his back to the front tire of the car. His gun rested on his lap, his finger against the outside of the trigger guard, the barrel aiming at Collins.

"Ya know, it's a little off-putting having ya point that thing at me when I'm trying to concentrate," said Collins.

The man stared back over the rims of his sunglasses. "And yet, I don't seem to give a damn."

Collins smiled dismissively. "Well, I bet ya were the popular kid in class, weren't ya? Prick."

He re-focused his gaze through the sights of the sniper rifle and completed another slow scan of the port, sweeping left to right, from the entrance to the docks, and back again. There was activity but nothing of any interest to him. He had committed the face of his target to memory, and there was no sign of anyone who didn't simply work there for a living.

Not yet anyway.

He looked over again at the man.

"What's your name?" he asked.

"Does it matter?" replied the man.

"I just figured we're gonna be spending a fair bit of time together. May as well make it amicable, right?"

The man smiled. "Why? You hoping to work together again or something?"

Collins chuckled. "Hell no. This is a one-and-done job for Patty. Just a bit of business we're taking care of, ya know?"

The man continued to smile. "Right..."

Collins held his gaze, processing his reaction before returning his attention to the scope. He concentrated on the task at hand, trying to remain calm. But a sickening realization had just dawned on him. The guy next to him wasn't just there to make sure he completed the job. He was there to tie up loose ends for Velasquez.

He was there to kill him.

15

The jet had been airborne a little over twenty minutes. Darius Silva had met them at the airfield, accompanied by three of his own personal bodyguards. After courteous greetings had been exchanged, everyone had hustled on board, anxious to take off.

The plane was from GlobaTech's own fleet. Gone were the days when they relied on the acquired assets of the people they fought against. It was painted white, with an orange and black tailfin that sported the image of a globe that had become one of the most recognizable symbols in the world. Inside offered seating for twenty passengers—ten comfortable reclining chairs on either side of the carpeted aisle, with plenty of space in between.

Jericho and Julie sat on either side of the aisle, with Hyatt and Silva opposite them. Silva's men had opted to sit toward the rear of the plane, away from the group.

Hyatt stared out of the small window, his face obscured by a mask of doubt and concern.

"Is everything okay, my friend?" asked Silva, noticing his expression.

Hyatt looked around but didn't get a chance to reply.

"No, he's not okay," said Jericho sharply.

Picking up on his tone, Julie reached over and placed a hand on his arm. "Don't..."

He shrugged her away. "No. I'm not going to sit here while this sonofabitch acts all nice and polite and innocent, as if nothing's happening."

"Excuse me?" said Silva, scowling. "You should watch your tone."

There was a sound of hurried movement, and Silva's bodyguards all appeared in the aisle alongside him, their hands hovering over their weapons.

"Is there a problem, sir?" one of them asked.

"No," he replied. "The hired help forgot their place, that's all."

Jericho rolled his eyes and smiled. "Hired help? Oh, I'm gonna enjoy this."

He leapt to his feet, followed a second later by Julie, who lunged to intervene before he could wrap one of his giant hands around Silva's throat. In a heartbeat, the noise of shuffling and clacking was audible over the roar of the engines as weapons were drawn and aimed. Jericho aimed at Silva. The bodyguard who spoke aimed at Jericho. Julie aimed at him. The remaining bodyguards covered the stand-off from a distance, ensuring everyone had a gun pointing at somebody.

Silva sat calmly, smiling at Jericho. "What are you going to do? Shoot me inside a pressurized cabin, fifteen thousand feet in the air?"

Jericho glared at him. "Don't tempt me, asshole."

"You should sit down."

"No, you should shut your damn mouth. We got hit last night because of you."

Silva's expression changed to one of surprise and skepticism. "What?"

Julie sighed. "Six armed cartel soldiers attacked our hotel. We took them out, but it was a bad situation."

Silva glanced at Hyatt, who was shifting uncomfortably in his seat, squirming at the sight of the guns. "Ulysses, are you all right?"

Hyatt nodded. "Y-yeah, I'm fine."

Silva turned back to Julie. "How did they know where you were staying?"

"Good question. A better one would be why they would risk hitting us in such a public place. We need to know what's going on. You need to tell us about this shipment, and why it's so important, because right now, the bad guys seem to know more than we do, and that makes our job very difficult."

Silva looked in turn at Julie and Jericho. He saw the unblinking eyes, the unwavering aim, the conviction etched onto their faces.

He went to speak but stopped himself.

Jericho sighed and took a step toward him, pressing the barrel of his gun against Silva's forehead. The color drained from Silva's face, but he still waved away his men when they bristled with retaliation.

"Now isn't the time for secrets," said Jericho. "This is where we are: we're going to land in Halifax in about an hour. When we do, your shipment is going to come and go, just like you want, and we're going to shoot anyone who shows up that didn't arrive on this plane. This is the end game, Darius. There's no need to keep us in the dark. We need to know what this is all about. Then maybe, just maybe, we can be proactive for once, instead of just dealing with shit going wrong."

Silva looked at his men and nodded. Reluctantly, they lowered their weapons and stepped away. A moment later, Julie did the same. Jericho waited a few seconds longer before removing the barrel of his weapon from Silva's forehead. Everyone returned to their seats, and silence fell inside the cabin, bringing with it a slow wave of calm.

Hyatt sighed loudly with relief.

Jericho gestured to Silva. "Well?"

Silva hesitated briefly before speaking.

"I am a businessman," he began, looking at Julie and Jericho in turn. "I have powerful and influential associates with whom I have cultivated strong and profitable relationships over many years. One of my associates is having some... difficulties, and they turned to me for help. A cargo ship coming from the South China Sea will be docking at the Port of Halifax in approximately..." He paused to check his watch. "...five hours' time, at which point a shipping container owned by one of my many legitimate enterprises will be loaded onto it. The container will not be registered on the ship's manifest. Inside it is sixteen million U.S. dollars in cash, belonging to a powerful and lucrative friend, who is paying me a nice percentage to launder it through my bank in the Caymans. However, should anything happen to his money while under my protection, he will become a powerful and well-funded enemy. As I am sure you will appreciate, I can ill afford to have this happen."

"So, that's what this shipment is?" asked Julie. "Millions of dollars in cash?"

Silva nodded. "In crisp, hundred-dollar bills."

"And that's why someone is trying to take it from you?" asked Jericho. "To turn your friends against you, which will weaken you and leave you vulnerable."

"Exactly," confirmed Silva. "So, can you see why this is so important?"

Julie nodded. "I can, but I don't understand why you need to involve Mr. Hyatt."

Silva shrugged. "He is my accountant. He is coordinating with the port and the bank to ensure the shipment is delivered securely. He also needs to check the bills in person to make sure they're not tagged, and to make sure the serial numbers are logged in such a way that suspicions aren't raised should the deposit be noticed by any federal agencies. He is invaluable to this entire arrangement."

Julie glanced at Hyatt, who smiled humorlessly and waved. "Hi."

"And you have no idea who could be behind this?" Jericho asked Silva. "Who could be working with the cartel?"

Silva thought for a moment and then shrugged. "Honestly, it could be any number of people. It's not uncommon for someone like me to make enemies."

"I can't imagine why. Once this is over and the ship leaves, we're getting Hyatt back on this jet ASAP and flying straight back to California. I'm sure you won't mind making your own travel arrangements?"

Silva smiled. "As frustrating as it may be, I have to admire the tenacity with which you approach your jobs. Were you anybody else, I would've had you killed and disposed of days ago for the way you've treated me."

Julie smiled back. "Lovely. Just so *you* know, if we weren't here protecting Mr. Hyatt but knew of your involvement in the Mexico incident, I'd have put a bullet in your head from a mile away days ago."

Silva laughed. "I find you rather pleasant company, Miss

Fisher. I really do. Very well. The ship will be arriving at Pier 9, where it will remain docked for two hours. A small window of concern for you both."

Julie looked over at Jericho, silently asking if he had any further questions. When he nodded his acceptance of the situation, she looked back to Silva. "Thank you for your cooperation. It will be considered, should our paths ever cross again."

Silva got up and moved to sit with his men. Jericho and Julie spent the remainder of the flight updating their own strategies with the information Silva had given them, triple-checking every eventuality they had planned for to ensure they're prepared for whatever might happen before the ship leaves for the Caymans.

The flight passed by quickly, and they were soon taxiing across the runway at a small, private airstrip not far from the port itself.

Julie stood and stretched before turning to Hyatt and tapping his leg with her foot. "Let's go, sunshine. Make sure you wear your big boy pants."

Jericho rolled his eyes and smiled at Hyatt as he stared blankly ahead. "What my colleague means is, it's time to go to work, Mr. Hyatt. This is where we earn our money. Just focus on what you need to do, so we can get you out of here and back to your daughter, okay?"

He nodded absently and headed for the exit, following Julie's lead. As Jericho stood, Silva stepped alongside him.

"You don't strike me as a natural diplomat, Mr. Stone," he mused.

Jericho looked down at him, his expression firm. "My colleague and I work well together because we take turns being nice and being cranky." He paused to crack his neck and flex his shoulders out to his full width. "My turn at being nice is almost over."

Sensing there was little benefit in responding, Silva quick-stepped toward the exit. He caught up with Hyatt as his men caught up with him, leaving Jericho at the back of the line, with a slight smile on his face.

16

Collins continued to gaze patiently through the scope of his rifle, not so much searching for his target but for a moment of inspiration that might get him off the roof of the parking garage alive.

He had yet to find one.

His babysitter was clever. He was far enough away to get a shot off should Collins lunge for him but close enough that he wouldn't need to aim for the shot to be fatal.

Collins knew he had to stall. His target could show up at any minute, and despite the fact the world would most likely be better off without Darius Silva in it, he didn't want to be the one to remove him from it. He was a good soldier and a bad gambler, but he wasn't a killer. His desperation forced him to offer his services to Velasquez in exchange for his life. However, given how unlikely it now appeared that he would remain alive anyway, he saw no reason to take the shot at all.

He didn't want to die with innocent—or at least unjustified—blood on his hands.

He had to stall.

He sat back on his haunches and rolled his shoulders, loosening the muscles to relieve some of the tension that had built up.

"Hey, don't take your eye off the target, asshole," said the man beside him.

Collins stared at him as if he had scraped him off the bottom of his boot. "Watch your tone, sunshine. My target ain't even here yet. I'm aching like ya wouldn't believe. Been an age since I sat behind a long gun, ya know?"

"I don't care. Do what you're being paid to do."

Collins chuckled. "Heh. Technically, I ain't being paid, so..."

The man raised his gun, putting the barrel level with Collins's eye. His finger tightened on the trigger. "Don't get smart. I ain't Patty, all right? I will not hesitate to shoot you and just do the job myself."

Collins grinned. *Got ya.*

"I tell ya, buddy, I don't think Miss Velasquez would appreciate ya callin' her Patty. Only people with special privileges get to call her that. If she finds out, there's no tellin' what she'll do to ya. Trust me."

The man smiled back. "I'm pretty sure she won't find out. *Trust me.* Now..." He pointed to the rifle. "Back to work."

Collins sighed and took up position behind the rifle again. He adjusted the focus of the scope and did another slow swipe, left to right, of the port.

———

Two Suburbans were parked at the end of the airstrip, nose to nose, their engines idling. Each one had a guard standing beside it. Jericho, Julie, Hyatt, Silva, and his three men made their way across the tarmac toward the vehicles. It was a short distance, which they all covered in a hurry, hastened by the nervous tension that had woven itself around them.

Without a word, Silva and his men climbed into the one on the left. Julie slid in behind the wheel of the other. Jericho got in beside her, and Hyatt took the rear seat. Silva's car reversed into position and then sped toward the exit. Julie did the same and kept pace as they headed for the port.

"You okay?" asked Julie, not taking her eyes off the road ahead.

"Yeah," replied Jericho. "Just running through everything."

"We got this. Did Buchanan get a hold of Ray?"

Jericho shook his head. "He hadn't the last time we spoke."

"Could've done with him on this one." When Jericho didn't respond, she glanced sideways to see him staring at her with a raised eyebrow. She rolled her eyes. "You ever tell him I said that, I'll deny it and shoot you. Maybe not in that order."

"My lips are sealed," he said, smiling.

Behind them, Hyatt allowed his head to roll back against the seat as he let out a long, pained breath.

"Oh, God, I'm going to die..." he whispered.

Kim Mitchell burst into Buchanan's office holding a small pile of papers in her hand. He had his head buried in paperwork but looked up, startled by her entrance. He quickly noted her expression. Her eyes were wide, her brow furrowed. She was breathing quickly. He could tell she came bearing something of grave importance.

"What is it, Kim?" he asked apprehensively.

"Sir, I think we've found Ray," she replied, slightly out of breath.

She moved to his side and placed the papers on top of the pile he had been reviewing, spreading them out. He glanced at them briefly.

"What am I looking at?"

"We were able to track the last location where his cell phone pinged a local tower," she began, sorting through the papers as she spoke. "Which was outside a hotel in Miami yesterday morning. The signal disappeared, but we... *acquired* access to the security feed of the hotel, which gave us this image."

She moved a black and white screenshot to the front, showing Collins standing beside his rental, surrounded by three men, with a fourth, much larger man on the ground.

"Who are these people?" asked Buchanan.

"We don't know, but we pulled the license plate of the vehicle they took Ray away in from another feed. We used traffic cameras and satellite footage to track them to a private airfield. A different vehicle left the airfield approximately thirty minutes later, but it's unknown if Ray was in it."

"So, where is he now?"

"Well, I asked the analysts to check all airports in the city, including private ones. I figured whoever he was with wouldn't keep him inside a private plane all day and night, so he must have gone somewhere. They ran facial recognition software through all airport security servers in Florida. That's when we found him."

She shuffled another picture to the top of the pile, showing Collins walking away from a ticket desk at Miami Airport, holding a cell phone in his hand.

Buchanan stared at the image. "When was this taken?"

"Thirteen hours ago. We used the time stamp of the security footage to cross reference the airport's booking systems, to see if we could find the ticket he purchased."

"And?"

"And this part I can't really explain." She paused to take a deep breath, unsure of the consequences of what she was about to say. "Sir... he was travelling to Halifax, Nova Scotia."

Buchanan looked up at her, his eyes wide with disbelief. "But that's where..." He stared at the photo again, giving himself chance to think clearly. "Right, this can't be a coincidence. But we know he's had no contact with Jericho or Julie as they would've said so." He tapped the image with his finger. "That cell phone he's holding... it can't be his."

Kim shook her head. "No, his number has been turned off for a while."

Buchanan flicked back to the picture taken outside the Miami hotel. He ran a trained eye over every inch of it before tapping it.

"There. By his feet. That could be a cell phone, right?"

Kim leaned in close and squinted, trying to make out the small detail in the photo.

"Hmm, possibly. You think someone destroyed his, then gave him a different one?"

"Maybe, yeah."

"But, why?"

"That's what we need to find out." He gathered the papers together and handed them back to Kim. "Try to trace the owner of the plane Collins was taken to after the hotel. That might give us some idea of who's behind his trip north of the border. Until we have proof to the contrary, we have to assume he's intending to rendezvous with Jericho and Julie in some capacity, but we can't rule out the possibility he's been compromised."

Kim gasped. "Sir, you can't think—"

He held up a hand. "I don't think Ray's gone to the dark side. Relax. But I do think he's travelling under duress. He didn't know the details of Hyatt's protection gig because he took some vacation time. The fact he's travelling there at all means that whoever has something over him might be involved with whatever Hyatt's got going on in Halifax."

"I'll get on to the analysts right away, sir."

"Good. Thank you. I need to get in touch with Jericho, give him a head's up before whatever shit is heading his way starts to hit the fan."

Kim left with the same urgency with which she entered. Buchanan reached for his phone and began to dial a number from memory.

Jericho's cell phone started ringing. The shrill tone filled the inside of the Suburban. He reached inside his jacket to retrieve it and answered on the third ring.

"Jericho."

"It's Buchanan," came the deep, gravelly response.

Jericho glanced sideways at Julie, who was staring questioningly at him, and mouthed *Moses* to her.

"Yes, sir?"

"Where are you?"

"Right now? We're following Hyatt's client, en route to the port."

"Okay. You might have a problem."

"Another one?"

"Collins landed in Halifax sometime in the last four hours."

"How is that a problem?" He paused, smiling to himself. "Beyond the obvious..."

"He's been compromised. My guess is he's there to kill Hyatt."

"I didn't catch that, sir. Say again?"

"You heard me, soldier," said Buchanan. "He was taken from his hotel in Miami yesterday. We think whoever took him is making him kill Hyatt. I can't think of any other reason why he would be travelling to Halifax."

"We've not had any contact with him."

"Neither have we. His cell phone was destroyed. He was given a burner phone by whoever took him. That's why we've been unable to reach him."

"What does this mean, sir?"

Buchanan sighed. "It means you and Fisher better watch your asses. I have no doubt Ray will do what he can, but if he's acting against his will, he may not have any options but to engage."

Jericho was silent for a moment.

"Understood," he said and hung up.

"What's going on?" quizzed Julie. "Is Ray coming to help?"

Jericho turned to her, a reluctant grimace on his face. "Not exactly."

Through his scope, Collins saw the large, electric gate guarding the entrance to the port slide open. A moment later, two black Chevy Suburbans rolled in. They moved across his view, past the warehouses and the container yard, before stopping outside the foreman's office.

"Aye, aye... this could be it," he muttered.

He glanced to the side and saw his babysitter kneeling beside him with a pair of binoculars held to his face.

"Is this the target?" he asked.

"Maybe..."

Collins watched him, sensing perhaps now was the time to make his move. He could secure his weapon and incapacitate the guy before he realized what had happened. He wouldn't need to fire a shot, and he could get away before Velasquez knew he was gone.

But he didn't make a move. Instead, he found himself questioning why the guy was suddenly so careless after being so calculated for so long.

The man lowered the binoculars and turned to Collins, smiling at his visible hesitation.

"I hope you're not getting any ideas?" he said. "Let me guess. You figured I'd let my guard down?"

Collins grinned sheepishly. "Heh. How'd ya guess?"

"Because you're the worst kind of transparent." He pointed over at the entrance ramp to the roof of the parking lot. "And because you don't see the bigger picture."

Collins looked over his shoulder to see three men standing across the mouth of the entrance, at the top of the ramp. Each one held a submachine gun that was strapped over their shoulders.

"Ya sneaky bastard..."

"Indeed. Now take your shot, Mr. Collins."

"Shite," he muttered under his breath.

He looked through the scope once more, refocusing on the two Suburbans. The first one stood with its doors open. Four men idled near the hood, seemingly deep in conversation. Collins looked on as the men shuffled together. Finally, they separated, giving him a clear view. His sights rested on Darius Silva.

"I see him," he announced.

"So, take the shot already."

"Just gimme a minute, would ya? There's another vehicle down there. I wanna see who's in it."

The man sighed. "Why?"

Collins looked across at him. "Because, dipshit, I'm a professional. The moment I pull the trigger, everyone who's down there and still alive is likely gonna start firing in our general direction. There's five of us now, right? Well, there could potentially be eight of them. Seven, not counting the guy I'm about to shoot. In the interest of avoiding being shot for as long as I can, I'd rather take out this douchebag once I understand what the consequences will be. Is that all right?"

The man gestured with his gun for Collins to hurry up. "Just get on with it."

Collins sighed and looked back through the scope. The other Suburban had stopped a little bit behind the first one. The driver's door stood open. He saw the back of a woman. Long hair. Trouser suit.

He squinted in the scope.

That ass looks really familiar, he thought. *It can't be...*

He watched as the passenger door opened, and Jericho Stone stepped out. He moved to the rear door and opened it. A moment later, Ulysses Hyatt emerged from the back seat, carrying a briefcase.

"No freakin' way..." he whispered.

He adjusted his view back to the driver. The woman had turned around. It was Julie Fisher.

"Ya have to be kiddin' me..." he whispered again.

"What is it?" asked the man beside him. "What's the delay?"

Collins rolled back on his haunches once more, moving away from the rifle and twisting to face his babysitter.

"Ya won't believe this, but I promise I ain't pullin' ya leg, okay?"

"What are you talking about?"

"My target... this Darius Silva bloke that Patty wants me to kill... he's standing down there right now with my teammates from GlobaTech."

"What? How? Why?"

Collins held his hands up. "Hey, ya got me, buddy."

The man trained his gun on Collins' forehead. "Did you do this? Did you call them here?"

"How could I? Only cell phone I have is the one your boss gave me. It's preprogrammed, so it can only dial her. I've had no way to get in touch with my friends. If I did, do ya not think I might've done it a little sooner?"

The man lowered his gun and looked through his binoculars again. "This isn't my problem. And it isn't Miss Velasquez's problem either. Do what you came here to do."

"I do that, and ya won't just have Silva's men coming for ya. It'll be GlobaTech's finest. Do ya know how bad that'll be for ya? Not wishing to blow my own horn or nothin', but me and my team... we're the best there is. Period. They'll kill every last one of ya."

He re-aimed his gun at Collins. "Figure it out."

Collins thought for a moment or two, trying to find a way to use this to his advantage. He looked back at the three men guarding the entrance to the roof. He thought how he hadn't heard them get into position. Then it hit him.

He looked back at his babysitter. "Lemme speak to them."

"What? Are you insane?"

Collins shrugged. "Possibly. But that's not the issue right now. If I can get my guys outta there, it will allow me to take out Silva without setting GlobaTech on ya ass." He held out his hand, gesturing for the man's cell phone. "Come on, we're running out of time."

The man reached for his phone and held it in his hand, staring for a moment before reluctantly handing it over.

"Anything I don't like, you're getting a bullet," he said. "No second chances."

Collins nodded. "No problem."

He began dialing.

In the port, Jericho and Julie stood on either side of Hyatt, scanning the area, hands loose and ready to draw their weapon. The wind blowing in from the North Atlantic Ocean took another few degrees off the already low temperature.

Julie shivered on the spot as she tried to relax. Away to her left, Silva and his men were standing around the hood of their Suburban.

"What are they waiting for?" she asked Hyatt, nodding toward the group.

Hyatt looked over and shrugged. "I... I don't know. Probably for the foreman to come out. Mr. Silva will want to remain discreet and keep this all as innocent as possible, to avoid any attention."

Before she could say anything else, her cell phone rang. She answered it quickly.

"Fisher."

"Hey, Kate, it's Ray."

Her eyes pinged open, and she looked over at Jericho with silent urgency. He saw the look in her eyes and nodded toward the phone. They stepped away from Hyatt and she placed it on speaker.

"Hey... Ray," she replied. "Everything okay?"

"Yeah, everything's great. I'm calling on behalf of Vinny. He can't come to the phone right now, but he sends his regards, ya know?"

"I hear you, Ray. Does he have a message for me?"

"Aye, he says he's in town for a party, and you're invited. Ya can bring a mate too, if ya want."

"Sounds great! Whereabouts? We'll be right there."

"Oh, not too far, love. I tell ya, we'll be having that drink ya like so much. The one with *port* and brandy in it. Anyway, I got a great view from Vinny's place. I can see the *ocean* from here. It's his usual spot. Ya know the one, right? Can't wait to see ya, Kate."

The line went dead.

"W-what was that about?" asked Hyatt, who had been listening.

Julie ignored him.

"What do you think?" she asked Jericho.

"Not sure. He said Vinny couldn't come to the phone right now, which is weird."

"W-why's that weird?" asked Hyatt, seemingly desperate to understand what was happening.

"We each have codenames," explained Julie. "For the others to use on an open line in case we're compromised. We think one of our colleagues has been sent here to kill you. That was him, but he said his codename couldn't talk."

Jericho snapped his fingers. "Whoever made him come here is with him, but they know him."

Julie nodded. "Right. That's why he couldn't use the fake

name. They know his real one, so it would've raised suspicions."

"He's watching us from somewhere right now," said Jericho. "But where? He said he had a great view..."

They each looked around the port. When nothing obvious presented itself, they began looking farther afield—to their right, out of the gates and across the street... to their left, out across the ocean, in case he was on a boat... and then directly ahead of them.

"There," said Julie. "That's got to be it."

Hyatt followed their gaze. He saw nothing except undeveloped land on the other side of some fencing that served as a border for the port. Beyond that was a low-level skyline of buildings, and...

"The parking garage?" he asked.

Jericho nodded. "Uh-huh."

"But that's... that's miles away!"

Jericho shrugged. "I'd say about a half-mile. Ray could easily make the shot from there with a long gun. He'll be on the roof."

Julie nodded. "I've got an idea. Wait here." She walked over to Silva, standing close to him and leaning in to speak in his ear. After a moment, he simply nodded, and she turned on her heels, heading for the Suburban. She climbed in quickly behind the wheel and gunned the engine. She spun it around, so she was facing the main gates and stopped in front of Jericho and Hyatt.

She buzzed the window down and leaned across. "Get in. I'll explain on the way."

They both did so without question, and she sped out of the port, leaving tire marks on the ground behind her and smoke in her rear view.

17

Collins watched them climb into the Suburban and speed away. He looked over at his babysitter. "I reckon that did it. They just left."

"Good," he replied. "Now you can get on with it, so we can all go home."

"Uh-huh..."

Collins got back into position and brought the sights to rest on the center of Silva's forehead. His finger rested gently on the trigger. His heart was beating hard against his chest.

I really hope that worked, he thought. *I'm out of time.*

He took his time, running through every pre-shot routine he could think three times over. Anything to steal another valuable second.

He sensed more movement to his left. A moment later, he felt the barrel of the gun press against his temple. He closed his eyes, silently cursing himself as he replayed every second from the last twenty-four hours that had led him to this situation in his head.

"What's the delay?" asked the man impatiently.

"Hey, will ya cut me some slack here?" replied Collins,

shrugging him away. "This is a difficult shot. I'm five-hundred-plus yards away, shooting into a strong crosswind, and it's not as if I can count on ya to give me an accurate spot, now, is it?"

"Again... not my problem."

"Aye, well, it will be if I miscalculate the shot and the bullet gets blown into the fuel tank of that big-ass Chevy, won't it? The fireworks'll be seen for miles and then a whole new kind of holy hell will rain down on ya. Now are ya gonna let me take my shot like a professional or not?"

Both men held each other's gaze for a long, tense minute before the babysitter looked away, waving at Collins dismissively.

"Whatever. Just get on with it."

"Thank you," he replied sarcastically.

He knelt still for another couple of minutes, lining up his shot perfectly until he knew, with absolute certainty, he would hit his target. But still, he waited. He needed to buy as much time as he could for—

He heard a noise behind him. It was faint. Muffled. But unmistakable. It was the sound of a body hitting the ground. Forgetting his situation, he looked over his right shoulder toward the entrance ramp. All three men were sprawled on the ground. Julie Fisher was standing over them, smiling. She waved casually.

Collins smiled back. As he turned toward his babysitter, he heard a loud bang. A second later, he felt something punch into his shoulder. Something small and hot. He felt his skin blister and tear. A sensation like lightning exploded along his arm, and he fell backward, as if dragged by a wild horse.

He clamped a hand over his shoulder where the bullet had struck him.

"Gah! God... *dammit!* Ya shot me, ya bastard!"

The man got to his feet, already swinging his gun around to take aim at Julie, a cell phone held to his ear.

Collins lifted his head to see. He wasn't sure where Julie was, but he knew the man wouldn't hesitate to pull the trigger. He lashed out with his leg, catching the guy in the knee and sending him off-balance. He staggered backward, dropping the phone but holding onto his weapon. Collins used the moment of reprieve to shuffle himself away, trying to get to his feet while keeping the pressure on his bullet wound.

The man recovered and stepped toward him, aiming his gun dead center at Collins' chest.

"I'm going to enjoy this, you irritating sonofabitch! Miss Velasquez sends her regards..."

Julie lunged forward, spear-tackling him as he pulled the trigger, dragging the bullet off-course. It chipped away at the concrete above Collins' head. He ducked anyway instinctively.

"Jesus! Watch it, will ya!"

Julie recovered quickly, kicked the gun out of the man's hand, and brought her foot down hard on the side of his head. He grunted as consciousness left him.

She dropped to one knee to catch her breath and then looked over at Collins.

"Where the hell have you been?" she asked.

He chuckled as he grimaced at his wound. "Did ya... miss me, love?"

She rolled her eyes and nodded toward his shoulder. "Does it hurt?"

He looked down at it. His hand was covered in his own blood. "Only a lot."

"Good. Get your ass up. You can explain everything in the car."

"Where are we going?"

She nudged the man on the ground with her foot. "I'm guessing your friend here was calling for back-up before I hit him, which probably means we're about to have a very bad day."

She helped him to his feet, and they walked as quickly as they could back down the ramp toward the Suburban. Collins climbed into the passenger seat. Seeing the vehicle was empty, he looked at Julie questioningly as she got in and started the engine.

"Where's Jerry and the other fella?" he asked. "I saw all three of ya get in..."

She nodded as she headed for the exit. "After you called, I figured you might have somebody with you watching, so we all left, but I let them out once we were clear of the port. They snuck back in over the fence a little farther along, where I figured you couldn't see."

"Nice."

She pulled out of the parking garage and sped back toward the port, weaving expertly between the other cars.

"We've got two minutes to get each other caught up," she said. "Start talking. Who wants Hyatt dead so badly that they would send you?"

He frowned. "Hyatt? Little Jessie's old man? Nah, I ain't here for him. I was sent to kill some fella named Silva. Darius Silva."

Julie glanced across at him, surprised. "Really? I wish I'd have known. I would've let you take your shot."

Collins laughed. "Bit of a prick, is he?"

"Just a bit. So, who hired you?"

"A woman named Patricia Velasquez. Nowadays, she's a big-time crime boss operating out of Miami."

"Nowadays?"

175

"Aye, I... kinda knew her way back when. We had a bit of a thing. Nothing serious, but... Listen, before I go on, will ya keep this between us?"

Intrigued, she nodded. "Yeah, of course."

"Thanks, pet. I owed someone a bit of money. A loan shark named Ramirez. I was into him for seventeen grand, to cover some gambling debts."

Julie sighed. "Oh, Ray... Jesus."

"Aye, I know, I know. Anyway, unbeknownst to me, Patty bought out my debt. Apparently, Ramirez was after my head on a spike, so she did it for old time's sake, as a favor, y'know? Thing is, she also hiked up the interest, meaning I ended up owing her three times what I owed the other guy. I couldn't pay it, so she had me do a job for her to clean my slate."

"Kill Silva..."

"Aye. I had no idea he had anything to do with Hyatt."

"I can't believe it..." she said, shaking her head. Then a thought popped into her head, and her eyes pinged wide. "Ray, I think this Velasquez woman is the one behind Jessie's kidnapping!"

"Huh?"

Julie navigated the traffic and turned right toward the entrance to the port. "I don't know. It makes sense. We got hit last night at our hotel. A group of cartel soldiers working for someone named Cortez."

"You're kidding?"

She shook her head. "No. Cortez is head of the cartel behind the kidnapping."

"Jesus. How are ya? Okay? And Jerry?"

"Yeah, we're all fine. They said they had been hired by someone working with their boss to steal a shipment belonging to Silva, and they had intel that said Hyatt was the key to doing that. It makes sense that it was this Patricia Velasquez, right?"

"Ah, I dunno, Jules. Patty's a lot of things—most of 'em bad, I admit—but hurting a little girl? I can't see it. What's the shipment?"

"Sixteen million dollars in cash, belonging to another scumbag who turned to Silva for help. If Velasquez takes that money from Silva, that puts him at war with his friends, weakening him in the process."

Collins stared blankly ahead, processing the idea that Velasquez could be capable of orchestrating the kidnapping of an eight-year-old girl. He didn't want to believe it, but he had to admit it made sense.

He growled loudly with frustration and used his good arm to slam his fist repeatedly against the dashboard in front of him, startling Julie.

"Bollocks!" he shouted. He sat back and took a deep breath, composing himself. "Okay, let's say you're right, and it *is* Patty behind all this. If taking the shipment makes the guy vulnerable, why send me to kill him as well?"

"Insurance, maybe? Who knows?" She drove through the gates and slammed to a halt beside Silva and his men. Jericho and Hyatt were with them. "But that's a problem for another day. Come on."

They climbed out of the car. Jericho moved around the hood to greet Collins.

"Ray, are you all right?" he asked, noticing his shoulder.

"Aye, I'm fine, Jerry. Just a flesh wound. T'rough and t'rough, ya know? All in a day's work." He nodded at Jericho's clothes—yesterday's suit with fresh blood stains. "Ya look like shite, matey."

"What can I say? It's... ah... it's been a rough couple of

days." Jericho gestured to Hyatt, who was stood beside him. "This is Mr. Hyatt, our client."

Collins nodded a courteous greeting. "Ya got a great little girl, Mr. Hyatt. Maybe once this is all over, ya take her on a nice vacation somewhere far away, yeah?"

Hyatt nodded silently.

Collins looked at Jericho and Julie in turn. "So... I can't leave ya alone for two minutes..."

They all exchanged glances before smiling and patting each other on the shoulder.

Collins winced as Jericho's giant hand clamped down on his bullet wound. "Ah! Watch it, big fella."

"Heh. Sorry about that, man."

Silva stepped into the group and cleared his throat. "Would someone mind telling me what the hell is going on here?"

Collins smiled. "Sorry. I'm forgetting my manners. The name's Ray Collins. I work with these two lovely people. I was actually just about to shoot ya in the head."

Silva's eyes went wide. "You were what?"

"Gonna shoot ya. From about a half-mile or so over there. Now listen. I've had a really bad day, and I'm not as patient and understanding as my colleagues here."

Silva scoffed but said nothing.

"I have a couple of questions for ya," Collins continued, still smiling but with an edge to his voice. "Either ya answer them honest, or I'm gonna blow your brains out right here and give this place a fresh lick of paint. We clear?"

Silva nodded uneasily, and his bodyguards shifted restlessly behind him.

Collins finally let go of his hand. "Good. Now do ya know Patty Velasquez?"

Silva thought for a moment. "I do, yes. Wait... is she... is she the one behind all this? Is she after my shipment?"

Collins patted the air in front of him with his good arm. "Slow down there, cowboy. She hired me to kill ya, yeah. Didn't mention anything about a shipment to me, but then she wasn't in much of a sharing mood when we last spoke. Do ya know if—"

The sound of screeching tires filled the air. Everybody spun around to face the entrance to the port in time to see half a million dollars' worth of BMW slide to a stop ten feet away from them. The cold sun reflected off the new paint job, briefly masking the identities of the four people who climbed out.

The clack of heels sounded as Patricia Velasquez walked confidently toward them, holding a small .22 caliber pistol low in her right hand. She wore a brilliant white dress, which clung to her figure in the best of ways, and a white, fluffy jacket that was short enough to just about cover her breasts. Behind her, three men in suits armed with assault rifles followed, aiming generally in the direction of the group.

"Ray, Ray, Ray..." she began as she approached them. "Do you have any idea how much I despise leaving Miami? Can you even *begin* to imagine in that tiny mind of yours how angry it makes me?"

Collins stepped toward her. "Patty? What are ya doing here? Listen, I—"

"I'll tell you," she said, cutting him off. "It makes me almost as angry as I get when I'm betrayed by someone I trust." She looked past him, toward Silva. "Darius."

He nodded back. "Patricia."

"I can't help but notice how you're still breathing..." She re-focused on Collins. "Why do you do this to yourself, Ray?

Seriously. I *knew* I couldn't trust you. I just knew it! That's why I followed you here. I figured I should keep an eye on you personally. Make sure you didn't try to run away and hide behind your friends at GlobaTech. Looks like I was right to doubt you."

Collins sighed. "Look, Patty..."

"No, *you* look! I tried to be nice about all this. I gave you every opportunity to pay what you owe, but you still took liberties, and now here we are."

Collins felt an eerie calm wash over him. He felt safe knowing his friends had his back and that Silva had his own protection, which could be useful. But that didn't matter to him. He didn't need their help to deal with this. He was simply so angry, it had numbed him.

"I know why ya sent me after this prick," he said quietly, gesturing over his shoulder to Silva. "Ya want this shipment of his, don't ya?"

Velasquez shrugged. "Not that it's any business of yours, but—"

"Did you do it?"

"Do what?" she asked, frowning.

"Pay some piece of shit cartel to kidnap Hyatt's daughter as leverage."

She went to speak but stopped herself and simply smiled. "Ray... do you really think I would—"

"Oh, would ya shut ya mouth for one goddamn second! I've had it up to here with ya *Queen B* act, all right?" Collins took another step toward her, forgetting the situation... forgetting himself... thinking only of the courageous young girl he carried out of a gunfight in Mexico. "Don't bullshit me, Patty! I ain't playin', okay? If ya had anything to do with what happened to that little girl, our past be damned and to hell with the consequences, I will shoot ya where ya fucking stand! Now tell me..." He pointed at Hyatt. "Did you have his daughter kidnapped?"

Collins watched her eyes. She looked over his shoulder at Hyatt, then back at him. Her lips curled into a small smile at one side. "I did what I had to."

Collins balled both hands into fists. His teeth ground together until his jaw ached. He didn't know how to process the anger currently erupting inside him.

Velasquez took a step toward him, tapping her gun against the outside of her leg. Behind her, the bodyguards followed, their fingers twitching over the triggers of their weapons.

"This is a dog-eat-dog world, Ray," she explained. "A girl's gotta do what a girl's gotta do to make it. Darius and I move in the same circles. We know the same people. We know how this works. If you want to get ahead... if you want more... sometimes, you have to do things you don't want to do. Unpleasant things that serve the greater good." She leaned to the side, glancing past Collins and looking at Silva. "No hard feelings, Darius. This isn't personal. I just want what you have. You've had your time."

Silva moved to Collins' side, wearing a politician's smile and exuding confidence with each breath. "Patricia, I don't know what you're hoping to achieve with all this, but you've accomplished nothing. Mr. Hyatt's daughter is safe. You don't have my shipment. And you're surrounded by operatives who work for GlobaTech Industries—who really don't require any introduction. I suggest you get in your rental and head back to Miami. Go back to topping up your tan and selling weed on street corners like the small-time hooker you really are."

His words hung in the air, amplified by a heavy silence. It was as if the tension had stopped the very air around them. Behind them, the tide was still. No birds flew overhead. Time itself had frozen.

And then everything changed.

A noise like a thunderclap shattered the silence, as if a whip crack had exploded a grenade. Collins tensed every inch of his body with shock. A whisper of smoke trailed from the barrel of the small gun in Velasquez's hand. He glanced to his side as Silva dropped to the ground with a muted thud. A small, dark hole in the middle of his forehead slowly began to drip blood onto his face.

He looked back at Velasquez, speechless.

"Well, *that* was dramatic," she said with a sigh. She looked beyond Collins at Silva's bodyguards, who shifted nervously on the spot, hesitating to use their guns. "Would you boys like a job?"

They looked at each other, silently asking themselves what they wanted to do next. After a moment, they walked over to Velasquez, each nodded to her, and then took their places beside her own men, turning to face Collins and raising their weapons.

"Good choice," said Velasquez. "Now, Ray... regarding your concerns about the little girl. That really wasn't anything personal. It was a necessary evil. A regrettable one but necessary."

She strode confidently past him toward the Suburban. Jericho and Julie stood side by side in front of Hyatt. She stopped before them and looked at each one in turn.

"My, my, my... you're a fine specimen, aren't you?" she said to Jericho. "I can guarantee you more money than GlobaTech, if you want a career change?"

Jericho raised an eyebrow. "Lady, you need to take a step back."

She smiled, bemused. "Oh, and why's that?"

He nodded to the men behind her. "Because you don't have enough back-up to make it past me and get to Hyatt."

She threw her head back, laughing. It was loud and exaggerated.

"Oh, my God, you are *just* like Ray!" She took a step back, allowing herself room to raise her gun again. She wasn't small, especially in heels, but Jericho still towered over her. The barrel was aimed high but pointed unwaveringly at his face. Her expression changed. "You're just as stubborn and just as stupid. Now, I want that shipment, and the way things stand, the only person still breathing who knows about it is standing behind you. So, move, or I'll shoot you."

Julie rolled her eyes and sighed. "Okay, that's it. I can't take it anymore." She stepped in front of Jericho, squaring up to Velasquez. She was an inch shorter. She stared at her with dead eyes and a set jaw. "Do you know what the problem is with people like you?"

Velasquez glared at her, adjusting her aim so the gun pressed against Julie's forehead. "Please, enlighten me."

"You don't see the big picture. You're so focused on your own little piece of the pie, you fail to see what really matters, which causes you to miss things that are important."

"Such as?"

Julie shrugged. "There are three things, actually. The first is loyalty. You would sell your soul to climb another rung on your ladder, desperate for more power. You don't have anyone except yourself, and you rely on money and fear to keep people in line. Whereas we stick together. Whatever your history with Ray is, it doesn't matter to us. An attack on him is an attack on us. On GlobaTech. That's a war you won't win, but you're too blind to see it."

Velasquez stared at her impassively. "Did you work on that little speech, or was it improvised? It was very good..."

"The second—"

"Oh, we're actually doing your list? Okay, but be quick. I have things to do..."

Julie ignored her. "The second is underestimating your enemy. You think you have some kind of hold over Ray, and that's fine. Honestly, getting into debt with people like you was pretty stupid, but if you think that man is still the same person you knew way back when, then you're sorely mistaken. You see, he's a GlobaTech operative. As am I and the big guy behind me. We're tasked with protecting Mr. Hyatt. Now that might not mean much to you, but I'll let you in on a secret."

Velasquez rolled her eyes. "Oh, please do..."

Julie smiled and tapped her ear. "You see these comms units? Not only do they allow operatives like me to communicate with anyone in GlobaTech tuned to the same frequency, but there's also a distress button on the battery unit that activates a GPS tracker, allowing the nearest GlobaTech site to pinpoint your location and send an extraction team."

That caused Velasquez's expression to alter slightly. Her eyes narrowed with concern and doubt. She didn't know how much of that was a bluff but knew it was a risk not to take it seriously. She knew she had enough firepower behind her to handle this situation. Short-term, she wasn't worried too much.

"And the third thing?" she asked.

Julie smiled. "The third thing is that you *drastically* underestimated me."

With a flash of movement, she ducked to her left and whipped her arm up, knocking Velasquez's gun high into the air. Then she grabbed her wrist and pushed her, twisting the weapon from her grip as Velasquez staggered backward on her heels. In a heartbeat, Julie had the .22 pointed at Velasquez.

A moment later, the mechanical rustling of six automatic rifles being aimed filled the air. Collins stepped away, joining his friends as they formed a line in front of Hyatt. The scene settled.

"You're all dead!" screamed Velasquez. She pointed at Hyatt, who had shrunk behind the three operatives with fear. "I want that shipment! Tell me where it is, or I'll skin your daughter alive and send you her body parts in the mail!"

"Patty!" snapped Collins. "Ain't no way you're having that shipment. And I promise ya, if ya even look at that little girl funny, I'm gonna—"

"You're gonna what, Ray? You don't have the balls to play in my league, so shut your mouth. I'll deal with you once I've dealt with your friends." She glanced over her shoulder. "Kill the bitch and the big one."

Both Jericho and Julie took a breath, standing their ground as they tensed, preparing for whatever might happen next. But Collins didn't. He relaxed and smiled.

"What are you grinning at?" asked Velasquez angrily.

"Oh, nothing..." he replied.

"Y'know what..." She glanced back again. "Kill him too!"

Collins laughed. "It's over, Patty. You're done."

"What do you mean, it's over? I have twice as many men as you." She nodded at Julie. "You think you can take everyone here out with that gun before you're dropped?"

Collins ignored her and continued laughing. Julie looked over, confused, but quickly realized why and began laughing with him.

JAMES P. SUMNER

"What are you all laughing at?" shouted Velasquez. She growled and stamped her foot with anger. "What is *wrong* with you people?"

Jericho relaxed and walked toward her, ignoring the armed guards completely.

"Jules was right," he said to her. "You don't see the big picture."

He casually pointed a finger like a gun, aimed it behind her and nodded in the same direction.

She frowned and followed the gesture. After a moment of confusion, she saw it. Her eyes widened. Her mouth opened. Panic flooded her entire body.

"No..."

"I'm afraid so," said Jericho. "You really should've paid more attention when Julie was talking."

The black helicopter grew from a dot on the horizon to a hovering beast above them in a matter of seconds. Rope lines dropped from the sky.

"What are you waiting for?" yelled Velasquez. "Shoot them!"

But her men didn't move. They stood watching, craning their necks to see ten armed GlobaTech operatives, dressed in full combat gear and armed with weapons that made their rifles look prehistoric, descend at a rapid pace. They landed expertly and moved with swift and practiced efficiency to form a tight perimeter around the scene.

Velasquez's men all dropped their weapons and held their hands up without being asked.

She watched in disgust. "What are you doing? Kill them! Kill them all!"

Julie stepped forward, pushing through the group in front of her. She tilted her head slightly to one side, smiled, and then planted a right cross firmly on Velasquez's jaw. She tumbled to the ground, stunned.

Julie loomed over her, smiling. "I did try to tell you."

Velasquez glared back but said nothing. A moment later, Jericho and Collins joined their colleague, looking down at the woman who had caused all the troubles they each had experienced in the last few days.

"And you!" she screamed at Collins. "You still owe me fifty thousand dollars. I swear, I'll—"

"Ah, give it a rest, would ya?" replied Collins.

Just then, Hyatt pushed his way through to join them. He crouched in front of Velasquez.

"How did you know?" he asked her.

She frowned. "What?"

"How did you know I knew anything about what Darius was doing?" he continued. "How did you know I even had a daughter?"

Jericho, Julie, and Collins exchanged glances and shrugged.

"That's a good question," said Jericho.

Velasquez went to speak, stopped herself, then sighed, resigning to the fact she had no move to make.

"Once I heard what Darius was doing, it was obvious he would need the help of someone like you. I asked around, found out who he paid to manage his books, and then..."

"Then what?" urged Hyatt.

"Then I bought somebody in your office. Put them on my payroll to spy on you."

Hyatt was shocked. His jaw hung loose as he processed what she had said. He almost fell backward but took a moment to compose himself.

"Who?" he asked.

Velasquez thought for a moment. "Ah, what's her name...? Sophie something."

"*Sophie?*"

He stepped away and placed a hand on his forehead.

"You know her?" asked Julie.

Hyatt nodded. "That's my secretary."

"The tall, attractive one who kept giving me the eye?" asked Jericho.

Hyatt nodded again.

Collins looked over and smiled. "Jerry... my man!"

Julie shot Jericho a look that could've turned him to stone. He swallowed hard and looked away.

"She is *so* fired," muttered Hyatt, moving to the back of the group.

Jericho stepped toward the leader of the GlobaTech unit now surrounding the scene, identified by the different-colored logo on his chest.

"Captain, thank you for coming so quickly."

The man nodded. "No problem, sir."

Jericho pointed to the six bodyguards. "Round them up and detain them. Then put in a call to the FBI and the RCMP, get them to secure the shipment once it arrives."

"Copy that."

He turned back to Hyatt. "You should come with me. I'll need to speak to the foreman and anyone else who works at the port who knew about what Silva was doing here."

"Then we can arrange for your little girl to fly up here to see you," added Julie.

"Th-thank you," said Hyatt. "Thank you both."

They left, leaving Velasquez staring up at Collins, nursing her aching jaw.

"So, where does this leave us?" she asked him.

Collins held her gaze. "It doesn't leave us anywhere. We're done, Patty. And so are you."

Her face was twisted with rage. She glared at him with dark eyes filled with a renewed hatred. "You'll pay for this, you sonofabitch!"

He placed a hand over his gunshot wound and sighed heavily. Now it was over, he didn't have enough energy left to hate her for what she had done.

"No, Patty, I won't."

Two members of the GlobaTech extraction team appeared beside him.

"Everything okay here, sir?" one of them asked.

"Aye, ya can take her," replied Collins. "Secure her with the others. I'm sure the FBI will want to talk to her."

The men scooped her up and frog-marched her to the other side of the port, to join the others.

Collins felt a hand on his good shoulder. He turned to see Julie standing there, smiling at him.

"You okay?" she asked.

"Aye, pet. Thanks. Ya kicked ass back there."

She stepped close and kissed his cheek. "You're family. Don't mention it."

With that, she walked over to join Jericho and the unit leader by the chopper. He smiled to himself as he watched her walk away the way a little brother would at his older sister—feeling proud and grateful to know her. As she joined up with Jericho, he saw her say something to someone and then point over at him. A moment later, a man in green coveralls came running toward him, holding what looked like a toolbox. As he drew nearer, Collins recognized the uniform. He was a GlobaTech field medic. He was tall and well-built, with short brown hair and a thin beard. Collins thought he looked more like a soldier than a doctor.

"What say we take a look at that arm of yours?" he said as he approached, nodding at Collins' shoulder. He was well-spoken and friendly; calm, despite the chaos surrounding them.

Collins smiled. "Aye, that'd be grand, if ya wouldn't mind?"

The medic ushered him over to the wall of a nearby building, out of the way, and gestured for him to sit on the ground. He then crouched beside him.

"It's just a flesh wound," he said. "You'll live."

Collins rolled his eyes. "That's a real shame—I was kinda lookin' forward to the rest."

The medic smiled. "Rough day?"

Collins let out a long sigh. "Buddy, ya have no idea..."

THE END

ACKNOWLEDGMENTS

This has been a challenging and exciting novel to write. The first third of this story was written back in 2015, and it's something I've always wanted to come back to. I just needed the right angle... the right reasons to finish bringing this story to life, and finally, I have.

As always, I didn't do this alone. While writing is a fundamentally solitary task, every author needs the right people around them to lean on, to ensure the end product is everything it can be.

I firstly want to say a huge thank you to my readers. Specifically, the fine folks in my VIP Facebook group. They've been with me every step of the way, giving me words of encouragement and support when I've needed them. They've seen all the ups and downs of my personal journey over the course of this last year and have stood by me and helped me through. I couldn't be more grateful to have them!

Behind every good author is a great editor. Coral worked hard to make sure this novel realized its full potential.

Anyone who makes me look this good deserves all the recognition they get!

Finally, to my good friend and fellow author, Adam Croft, for giving me a much-needed kick up the ass on a daily basis, for helping me keep my eyes on the big picture, and for reminding me how lucky I am to be doing this for a living.

Thank you, everyone. This novel was for all of you.

EPILOGUE

The black Suburban pulled to a stop outside the steps of Hyatt's office building. Jericho was behind the wheel, his elbow casually resting on the edge of the door. Beside him, Collins was slouched in his seat, one foot resting up on the dash. His arm was in a sling. The bandage covering his shoulder was obscured by his jacket.

In the back, Julie sat half-turned in her seat, so she could see Jericho and Hyatt. He was sitting next to her, nervously drumming his fingers on the briefcase resting on his lap.

"Are you sure you're ready for this?" she asked Hyatt.

He took a long, deep breath, his shoulders rising with the intake and slumping as he exhaled. After a moment, he nodded and turned to her.

"Yes, I am. I need to carry on. Business as usual and all that. It's over now, so the best thing I can do is put it all behind me." He paused, narrowing his eyes. "It... *is* over now, isn't it?"

Julie smiled. "It is. And all things considered, you did pretty well, Mr. Hyatt."

He smiled back. "Thank you. What... ah... what's happened to Mr. Silva's shipment?"

Julie glanced forward, catching Jericho's gaze in the rearview. He nodded almost imperceptibly to her. She turned her attention back to Hyatt.

"It's been confiscated by GlobaTech," she said. "There's a unit guarding it at the port right now. We will work with the RCMP to investigate both Silva and Patricia Velasquez, as well as the foreman at the docks who was arranging for the shipment to be transported to the Caymans."

Hyatt sighed. "So, are you and Jericho heading back to the States now?"

"We're flying back later today, yes. Our boss has secured the private jet for us. Commercial planes don't agree with my colleague."

In the front, Jericho sighed. "They're too small. I hate sitting uncomfortably for so long. It makes me cranky."

Julie rolled her eyes at Hyatt and smiled. "See?"

Collins twisted in his seat. "Hey, hey, cut the man a little slack, would ya? I mean, look at the size of him! They should have special seats or something. Hardly fair, if ya ask me."

Jericho nodded. "You're right. Thanks, man."

They bumped fists.

Julie groaned. "Oh, for the love of... you two are as bad as each other." She looked at Hyatt. "Come on, I'll walk you to your office."

He looked surprised. "Oh, I thought your job was finished now? You don't have to—"

"No, it's fine. I want to. Just a couple of loose ends to tie up before we head back." She leaned forward and patted Jericho's shoulder. "I'll be five minutes."

"Take your time," he said, smiling.

Hyatt and Julie got out of the car and headed for the office.

"What's she doing?" asked Collins, gesturing with his head to the pair of them as they climbed the steps. "And why are ya smiling?"

Jericho glanced at him, still grinning. "I've a pretty good idea what her loose ends are."

After passing through the security checkpoint in the lobby, Hyatt and Julie had called the elevator and were riding it up to the fourteenth floor.

Hyatt shifted his weight back and forth and constantly ran a hand over his beard and hair, appearing restless.

"Is everything okay?" asked Julie.

He nodded. "Yes..." He shook his head. "No. No, it isn't. With that Velasquez woman in custody, I'm worried my name will be mentioned and then my career will be over. I trusted Darius, but her..."

Julie held up her hand. "Mr. Hyatt, relax. Take a breath. You'll be fine. Velasquez won't say or do anything for two reasons. One, anything she admits to knowing about what was happening at the port immediately incriminates her, which she'll want to avoid. And two, if she even looks at Montreal on a map, she fully understands what I'll do to her. Now just remember, if anyone asks where you've been, say you had a family emergency. Okay?"

Hyatt let slip a small smile. "Yes. Thank you." He sighed again. "Then there's the matter of my secretary. Velasquez said she was paying Sophie to spy on me. I have to fire her, but I need a valid reason. Otherwise, I'll have Human Resources and lawyers and God knows who else crawling up my ass. Except I can't cite the real reason because the company doesn't know about my other portfolio of clients, so again..."

Julie placed a hand on his arm, hoping it would offer some comfort.

"Well, maybe I can help with that situation, too."

The elevator pinged as the doors slid open. They stepped out into the reception area side by side and headed left, along the corridor toward Hyatt's office. His secretary's desk was on the right-hand side, not quite facing the elevators.

Sophie spotted them as they exited the lift and quickly buried her head in her keyboard. Julie noticed and smiled to herself.

Nowhere to hide, bitch.

As they drew level with the desk, Julie took a small step toward it, away from Hyatt. In a lightning-fast movement, she grabbed a hold of the monitor and ripped it away from the desk, tossing it away to her right. Sophie bolted upright in her seat, her eyes and mouth wide open in shock. Hyatt jumped with fright at the sudden noise, dropping his briefcase.

Without pausing, Julie leaned over and grabbed Sophie by her hair, then slammed her face into the desk. She lifted her up again and twisted her grip, forcing Sophie to look up and turn her head to alleviate some of the pressure.

Julie stared at her. She wasn't angry. She wasn't disappointed. She wasn't... anything. She felt nothing for the woman sitting before her. She examined Sophie's face. Her eyes were half-open and glazed. Her nose was busted open and bleeding. Her mouth hung loose, gasping for air.

"We both know why I did that," said Julie. "So, let's dispense with the formalities. In the next ten minutes, you will personally hand Mr. Hyatt a letter of resignation, which will include a sincere and detailed apology for your part in what's happened over the last seventy-two hours. Then you'll take your broken face and your wannabe beach bunny ass and walk out of here without looking back. Are we clear?"

Sophie nodded as much as she could under the circumstances.

Julie smiled. "Good."

She let go of her hair, and Sophie fell forward, slumping over her keyboard.

Julie turned to Hyatt. "You take care of yourself, okay? The second I get back to California, I will personally arrange a flight for your daughter to come out to you, escorted by someone I handpick for the assignment."

Hyatt stared in shock at his now-former secretary for a moment, unable to speak. Finally, he swallowed hard and turned to Julie, nodding.

"Th-thank you," he said. "Thank you!"

Julie smiled and walked back to the elevator. Two minutes later, she slid into the Suburban behind Jericho.

He glanced over his shoulder as he started the engine. "Are we done?"

She took a long, refreshing breath and leaned back in her seat. "We're done. Let's go home, boys. Drinks are on you two."

Jericho and Collins exchanged a quick glance, then all three began laughing as they eased out into the morning traffic, heading for their ride home.

A MESSAGE

Dear Reader,

Thank you for purchasing my book. If you enjoyed reading it, it would mean a lot to me if you could spare thirty seconds to leave an honest review. For independent authors like me, one review makes a world of difference!

If you want to get in touch, please visit my website, where you can contact me directly, either via e-mail or social media.

Until next time...

James P. Sumner

JOIN THE MAILING LIST

Why not sign up for James P. Sumner's spam-free newsletter, and stay up-to-date with the latest news, promotions, and new releases?

In exchange for your support, you will receive a **FREE** copy of the prequel novella, *A Hero of War*, which tells the story of a young Adrian, newly recruited to the U.S. Army at the beginning of the Gulf War.

Previously available on Amazon, this title is now exclusive to the author's website. But you have the opportunity to read it for free!

Interested? Simply visit the below link to sign up and claim your free gift!

smarturl.it/jpssignup

EPILOGUE

The only sound was of the ocean's lazy tide lapping against the sides of the dock. A large cargo ship stood alone and still and deserted, its huge shape casting many shadows that stretched out across the port.

Moonlight shone through the window of the foreman's office, illuminating the dead bodies with its eerie, pale glow. There were six in total, all stacked neatly in one corner. The GlobaTech logos had been ripped from their clothes. Each one had a matching bullet hole in the center of the forehead.

Four men moved quickly and efficiently in a tight, diamond formation, their fingers hovering over the triggers of their submachine guns. They were dressed in black from head to toe, their faces obscured by half-masks painted with skulls. Their steps were light. They moved like ghosts, silent and deadly, despite knowing with complete certainty there was no one around to spot them.

They navigated the maze-like layout of the storage yard, taking the rehearsed route of lefts and rights until they reached their destination.

Container PHDS16CI.

The man at the front of the diamond held up a fist, signaling for his team to stop and hold steady. He glanced over his shoulder.

"This is it," he said. "Let's move. Sixty seconds."

One of the men behind him stepped forward and produced a key taken from the foreman's office. He removed the padlock and lifted the bolts, then stepped aside as he pulled open the large container doors. The remaining two men moved in, stepping around three large, black, sports bags placed neatly in the middle of the huge space. The man from the front stepped inside and crouched next to one of the bags. He unzipped it and pulled it open. Inside, stored in neat, even piles, were blocks of hundred-dollar bills. He quickly closed it again and stepped outside, nodding to the man with the keys.

"Let's go. Thirty seconds."

The man nodded back, stepped inside, and picked up one of the bags. The other two men did the same.

"Twenty seconds," said the man in front. "Time to go."

Back in formation, they ran back through the maze of containers and across the dockyard, toward a black van waiting near the gates covering the entrance.

The bags were placed carefully in the back and then all four men climbed inside. The engine started up, and the van drove through the open gates, passing the two dead security guards in the hut to the side of them before disappearing into the light traffic of the evening.

The man from the front took out a cell phone and dialed a number from memory. When it was answered, he simply said, "We have the package."

Without waiting for a response, he terminated the call and tossed the phone out of the window. They turned onto the freeway, accelerating away from the ocean, disappearing into the night like ghosts.